Chasing Denver

RACHEL ANNE JONES

I dedicate this book to all my friends, family, and co-workers, who know how big of a broom is sometimes needed to sweep up my best intentions.

I also dedicate this book to afternoons spent with Amanda and Nathan in abandoned buildings in no-name ghost towns, and to anyone who ever has ever wondered what was in the locked briefcase.

"I think, I think when it's all over it just comes back it just comes back in flashes you know? It's like a kaleidoscope of memories; it just all comes back. But he never does... the crazy thing is, I don't know if I'm ever going to feel that way again. But I don't know if I should... I think that the worst part of it all wasn't losing him. It was losing me."

— Taylor Swift

1

My name was not important. My life was not important. I was not important, and I could live with being invisible, or so I thought. Being a nobody never bothered me, until I was singled out as a somebody, and that's when I discovered being known is not always better than being left alone.

My name is Ciara Onyx Yengst. I live in a nondescript town filled with ordinary people, a place I used to think was as dull as the endless supply of number two pencils I hoard in my desk drawer in my room, as I have always been a studious, prepared student. Schoolwork is the one area of my life I can control, at which I excel.

Denver Evans, on the other hand, is another matter. It has puzzled me more than once over the past few years, as I am an analytical person; how a sensible, level-headed, strawberry blonde, freckle faced girl like me could fall for a boy named Denver, who is as unpredictable and rocky as his first name. I'm still working on that equation, because me liking Denver makes about as much sense as an imaginary number. I don't know why I think I need him, but I can't seem to stop. The trouble started the first day we met.

I was twelve and he was thirteen, though I didn't know his age the day he showed up on my doorstep, dropping his red dirt bike on my lawn, walking over to the hose that still had water dripping from it. I had just finished watering my mom's flowers. He picked it up and took a few sips before stepping underneath the water, letting it flow down his front. Afterwards he plopped down on the porch step beside me with his clothes soaked to the skin, stirring feelings I didn't recognize or know what to do with, as he threw his arm casually over his knee, wiped his face on the back of his hand, and smiled up at me with a perfect pair of devastating hazel eyes.

"Hi. I'm Denver."

He stuck out his hand, dripping with water and sweat, covered in callouses that scratched my palm as he touched it. I was so tongue-tied I could barely get the words out as he held my hand in his. "I'm Ciara."

He pulled his hand back, and I almost died as I saw there, on the tip of his thumb, was a bit of brownie batter. I glanced down at my hands, shocked to see a bit still on me. He looked at his thumb in question before nipping it with his teeth. He looked back at me. "I'm glad that was chocolate." I didn't know what to say. I couldn't stop staring at his thumb. "Got any cards?"

"What?" His voice in my ears was as perfect as the rest of him.

"Playing cards. Do you have any?"

"Yeah." I'd never been so close to a boy before, at least not one that meant anything, and especially not one this cute. Why was he still talking to me?

"You going to go get them?"

"Oh, sure." I ran back inside and headed for the game room. My heart raced as I wiped my hands on my shorts. I remember running back through the front door, certain he would be gone, if he had ever been there to begin with, but there he sat, with his dark, curly hair and big green eyes that twinkled just right. We played cards all afternoon, and somewhere in there I got the courage to invite him in for some lemonade and a brownie.

We stood in the kitchen. He laid his plate down on the table before he walked over to me. He was tall for a thirteen-year-old boy, and unlike any boy I'd met before. He took my hand in his and weaved his fingers in between mine. It felt so strange. I didn't know what to say. The room got really warm, like I was standing too close to a hot oven. I was trying to decide if I wanted my hand back when he leaned in and whispered, as if we were playing a game. "Ciara, have you ever been kissed?"

I shook my head in answer, unable to speak while I stared at the floor, too terrified to look him in the eye.

I felt like someone else as he put his hand under my chin and gently pushed upward. My eyes looked into his and they got stuck there, remaining wide open, until his soft pink lips touched mine. Only then did my eyes close. I could barely breathe as he stepped back, giving me a big toothy grin.

"Now you have." He winked at me and snagged another brownie. Then he turned around and walked right out my front door, leaving me standing by the kitchen sink, my fingers on my lips, wondering if any of it was real.

And that was the first secret between me and Denver Evans.

———

Fast forward to the present. I am now sixteen and the ever-present Denver who never quite leaves my mind or radar is seventeen. My school-girl crush has grown into a case of full-fledged lusting after Denver with his unruly hair and devil-may-care style; having traded his elementary school red dirt bike in for a smokin' hot black motorcycle that runs on a good day.

He still leaves his bike on our front lawn quite frequently, much to the irritation of my older sister, Char, the nurse, and sole caretaker of our family now that my parents have been gone two years, courtesy of a drunk driver on the highway not even a mile from our home. If Char knows about my crushing on Denver, she's kind enough to not mention it, just as I don't mention her crazy on-and-off again thing going with her old high-school boyfriend, Cary, the ex-con turned Sheriff's best friend who spends every waking moment working in his garage on his totally drool-worthy Super Sport Chevelle.

It's a good thing Cary has a reliable Ford Ranger to haul his mower down to our house about once a week, a pathetic and contrived excuse to shamelessly peacock shirtless in front of Char, but my brother and I don't complain, as it's one less house chore we have to do.

Denver still plays cards at our house quite often, but I'm no longer his partner. He prefers to hang out with my annoying older brother, Crandall, better known as Crash. I imagine it has something to do with the fact that Crash keeps a steady supply of beer in his mini fridge in the apartment above our garage. This would also explain the regular presence of our neighbor down the way, Tom, buyer of said beer who's over the age of twenty-one, while my brother Crash is not. Tom is a kind of wandering loner who prefers to hide behind a set of head-phones. Sometimes I wonder if there's any sound coming out of them, or if he just likes the barrier between himself and the rest of the world.

Maybe I should buy some headphones, as it would save me from this excruciating group FaceTime conversation I'm enduring at the moment. I'm listening to another disgustingly detailed account of Gabi and Denver's latest makeout sesh, waiting for someone to mercifully change the subject and bring it to an end. I can't be the one, as Gabi will most likely set her sights on me, demanding to know why I *don't* want to hear all about how Denver is such a good kisser; how his hands are so skilled, and it was sooo hot. I struggle to keep my face blank as she goes on and on. "Ciara." Gabi's loud voice pierces my eardrum.

I reorient. "I'm sorry, what?"

"We're *talking* about the upcoming Winter formal. Who are you going with?"

I fail to hide my irritation as I answer, sighing. "I don't know. I mean, school just started. It's barely been a week."

Gabi sighs, all dramatic. "I know, but you *don't* want to go single *again*."

I shrug my shoulders. "It wasn't so bad." It was awful and humiliating. I was the only girl in my class without a date, and the only thing that saved the night from being a total disaster was Denver dancing with me on the second to last dance because Gabi was out in the hallway, cornering another unsuspecting victim with accusations of chasing after Denver.

Ari jumps in, saving me. "Sooo, what do you think of the new science teacher, Mr. Marro?"

I smile, getting excited. "I really like him. You can just tell he loves education."

Gabi rolls her eyes, which I mostly ignore. Magda pops back in the picture, holding a cookie in her oven-mitted hand. "Look guys! I made a cappuccino choc chip sandwich cookie. I can totally smell the coffee."

Ari answers. "Ooh, coffee! Looks delicious. Well, I'm going to get back to studying for our first English quiz. I've got some reading to do."

Gabi snorts. "You do that. While you're at it, can you type up a chapter summary and send it to me?"

Magda laughs. "Me, too."

Ari sticks out her tongue. "That's a negative."

Esmee pops up on the screen. "Hey, guys. Sorry I'm late. I was running Diamond down the lane. She gets antsy if I don't ride her every day."

Ari smiles into the camera. "Esmee, how was your last rodeo?"

"I did alright. Diamond did the best at the barrels."

Gabi frowns. "I wonder where Denver is? I've texted him like three times in the last thirty minutes but he's not answering."

Oh, boy. He's been over here for forty-two minutes, but who's counting. I hear footsteps on the stairs and my name being called. Gabi's eyes narrow. "Is that..."

I hang up the phone, stuff it in a drawer, and almost fall off my bed as I plop down on it as Denver steps into my room. "Hey." His easygoing manner is nowhere to be found. Something is definitely off, and the air is charged. I don't want to know, but I *have* to know. I try to act casual, but it's a challenge. Mega hot boy is in my room. This has never happened before. I pray my cheeks aren't flushed. I look up, and he's staring at me. I cough.

"Denver. What's up?"

"Were you just talking to Gabi?" *Why is he asking me this?*

"Not *just* Gabi." Why do I feel defensive?

"Did you tell her I was here?" *Again, why is he asking me this?*

I can't believe I'm flirting with him about his girlfriend. "She *is* your girlfriend."

He gives a shiver. "Don't remind me."

I tear my eyes from his face, skimming over his body parts before looking off sideways, recalling the conversation I just heard about his lips, his hands, and other things. I avoid his gaze, muttering, "It's kind of hard to forget."

He plops down in my orange fuzzy chair, sits deep in the middle, and spreads his knees wide. He runs his hands through his hair, devastating me. "What's that?"

I shake my head and look down at the ground. "Nothing."

He leans forward with his elbows on his knees, pops his head up, and levels me with his beautiful stare. "Ciara?" He could say my name all day long.

I return his gaze, paste on a small smile, and pray it doesn't reveal my undying devotion. "Yes?"

"Did you tell Gabi I was here?" *The boy's a broken record.*

"No."

He gives me a frown and what looks like disappointment before answering. "Thanks." That's weird. It seems like he wanted me to, but why?

I'm annoyed at my confusion in his tone and my own feelings I'm trying to ignore. "I didn't do it for you. I did it for Gabi." And for me.

"I didn't want to hurt her feelings." I didn't want to risk her wrath, and there's something delicious and thrilling about him being here and not telling her, but I'm trying not to think about that now.

He nods his head again, looking distracted. "Of course."

I search his face, trying to read him, but it's impossible. "Denver, are you okay?"

He sits in the chair for so still and so long, I think he'll never answer, as he stares down at his hands. He clears his throat. "Ciara, did you ever tell anyone about the day we met?"

My face heats up and I know I'm blushing, thinking about our kiss, the only one I've ever had. "No."

He gets up and shuts my door and then sits beside me on the bed. His hip rests against mine. "Ciara?"

"Yes."

"Things are going to change soon, and I need you to trust me, and keep your distance." His eyes look sad, like he might cry, and instinctively I reach for his hand, surprising us both. His eyes meet mine, and he leans in. Unlike last time, I meet him halfway, and for a few minutes, it's complete madness. By the time I gather my senses, we're both standing, and I'm plastered to his body. My hands are in his shirt. I pull away from him, scorched through and embarrassed. I may as well have jumped him.

"I'm sorry. I..." My fingertips touch my lips once more, and I'm twelve years old again.

He takes a deep breath, tilts my chin upward, just like before, and our eyes meet. As I look up at him, I hope I'm not the only one drowning in the new awareness between us that wasn't there before.

"Promise me from here on out, we're strangers. I don't want you to get hurt."

It's too late for that. I want to ask questions, but I can't speak. I numbly nod my head as he shoves his hands in his pockets, looking very much like the thirteen-year-old boy from not so long ago, as he gives me a shy grin. "Hey. Don't forget the first day we met, okay?"

He turns around, shuffles out my door, and closes it quietly behind him as I whisper after him, "How could I?"

My phone's going off like crazy in my drawer, but I leave it there as I plop back on my bed, shell-shocked and reeling from another encounter with Denver Evans, who remains as hot and mysterious as ever, and the first boy to ever own my heart.

─────

I spend the next two hours sitting at my windowpane, trying to read an assigned English novel while keeping a steady eye on the garage. Just about the time I think Denver will never leave, he and Crash walk down the steps and Denver gets in the truck with Crash. I ignore all the red flags in my head as I make a beeline for my brother's apartment, digging through his things like a maniac, not knowing what I'm looking for, and hating myself for practically sniffing the air for traces of Denver, but what was he talking about? What kind of trouble is he in? I know I've got it bad when I plop down in the beanbag, imagining Denver was just here, and my hands are resting where his have been, as this beanbag has his scent all over it.

It's while I'm settling in, leaning this way and that like a deranged cat checking its territory, that I see a misplaced object inside my brother's bag. If I didn't know better, I'd say it's Tom's signature Walkman, but what's it doing here?

I don't want to touch it, but I have to. I feel like I'm invading someone's personal space as I put the headphones on my ears, ready to satisfy my curiosity about what Tom's always jamming out to. I kind of envy his carefree walk as he bops along down the sidewalk so freely, oblivious to the curious looks of people passing by.

I push play, but nothing happens. That's weird. I hit the eject button. I'm stunned to pull out a hollowed-out cassette tape stuffed with little white pills. This isn't good. I flip the player over with shaking hands and open up the battery compartment, only to find more pills. I drop the tape on the floor, all shook up. I freeze as I hear my brother's truck pull back into the driveway. I shove the pills in my hoodie pocket before closing the Walkman and stuffing it in the back corner of Crash's duffel bag. I'm frozen for a few seconds as I hear footsteps on the stairs. I jump up, pace, and talk to myself. "Think, Ciara, think."

My brother opens the apartment door just as I pop my head up above the fridge. "Oh, hey Crash. I felt like a... beer..." the words feel foreign on my lips as I grab one from the fridge and round the island corner. I head for my brother's front door with my head down to avoid eye contact.

Crash doesn't answer, which is not unusual for him. I keep going and open his door to step outside, glancing back at him when I run into a solid body. The familiar scent betrays him, as Denver's hand

7

covers mine. He takes my beer and brushes my front while smirking down at me; and I wonder if I'm the only one who's every nerve ending tingles with anticipation.

"Ciara." He puts the beer to his lips, tilts his head back to take a long swallow before handing it back to me, half-empty. "Thanks."

I look up at him, remembering his last words to me hours before, as I utter his name like a curse word. "Bye, Evans."

I run back to my house, frantic, feeling like I'm carrying 100 pounds.

I dig through kitchen drawers and try to make the right decision. The old roll of flamingo-checkered duct tape does it for me, as well as the big Ziplock bag lying on the counter. I grab both before running to my room. I make short work of throwing all the pills in the bag, pushing all the air out of it before sealing it and then wrapping it with endless amounts of duct tape. Satisfied, I shove it back in my hoodie and run outside to my bicycle.

I start down the trail, determined to get to the river before dark. I hop off my bike, run down to the water's edge in my flip flops, and kick them off at the edge of the rocks. This gives me another idea as I feel a second bag in my pocket. I whip it out and throw the Ziplock inside, before stuffing as many rocks as possible in and sealing the second bag. I pause and pick up a long walking stick to test the waters before wading out into the river current. I search for the deepest part before tossing the bag in. I hope it finds the bottom and lodges itself there to become part of the river, like Denver has managed to do to me.

2

I get back to the house after dark and head straight for my room. I'm barely in the door, and someone grabs my hand. I swing out wildly, before I'm quickly taken to the floor, effectively pinned by someone sniffing my neck. "Denver?"

A light flips on, and I look sideways and see my brother's red face. He's ticked. "Get off my sister." Denver hops off and sits on my bed. "Get off my sister's..."

I cut him off. "Crash. What are you two doing in my room?"

He looks at me hard, as if he's trying to figure something out. "What were you doing in my apartment?"

"I told you. Looking for a beer."

"I don't believe you."

"I don't care." I ground the words out.

Denver gets between us. "Stop it, guys." He turns to me, studying my face. "We're looking for something."

I focus on keeping my face blank. "What is it?"

Denver bites his lip, and I struggle to keep my eyes off his mouth. "It's..."

Crash grabs him by the arm. "Sorry we were in your room, Ciara. Just forget it."

The two of them walk out, and I sit down, shaken. Whatever is going on, they are in it together. Char pops her head in. "Ciara, you going to wash those dishes?"

I nod my head, thankful for normal. "Yep. Sorry, Char, I forgot. I'll do them now." I wander downstairs, happy for mindless housework.

Char musses my hair. "Thanks, kid. I'm going to bed. I've got an early shift."

I frown. "Didn't you just get home?"

She sighs. "I pulled a double. Someone called in sick again."

My stomach churns with worry and irritation. I'm never working in a nursing home. "You gotta quit doin' that. You'll get overtired."

She laughs. "That's what Cary says. Don't worry. I know when to slow down. Besides, it's good money."

I feel guilty. "I can always get a job, Char."

She claps her hands at me. "Nonsense. Crash has one, and he pays rent. That helps out a lot."

I take a deep breath. "Char. About Crash. He's…"

I look back at her, notice the bags under her eyes, and her shoulders sinking as she looks exhausted and concerned. "What about Crash?"

I clear my throat. "Oh, nothing. I forgot what I was going to say." I turn back to my dishes, and she waits a few seconds longer. I remain silent.

Five minutes later, I hear footsteps in the kitchen, and I turn to open up to Char, but it's Crash. He walks up beside me and starts rinsing the dishes. "Hey."

I almost choke. "Hey."

"You about done here because I have something to show you." I don't want to know, but he's my brother. "Sure." I wipe my hands on the kitchen towel and go to the living room to sit, but he motions me upstairs. We enter my room, and he sits down and gets out his phone. "Just listen."

I hear Tom's goofy sing-song voice, but then soon there's another voice, and it's so sinister, I get the shivers. "Who's that?"

His eyes are wide as he looks at me. "That's Walkman."

I shake my head in disbelief. "Crash, his name is Tom. You know I don't like you calling him Walkman, and it can't be him."

His face turns red with irritation. My brother flushes easily. "Yes, it is, Ciara. I know. I was just there."

I fidget nervously. "Why were you recording him?"

"It was an accident, okay? These stupid touch screen phones are so touchy, and it was in my pocket, and I must have hit the wrong thing, but I'm glad I did, considering."

I look at him again. "What are you going to do?"

He slams his phone in my hand. "Ciara, please listen to the whole conversation. I need your help."

I sit on the side of the bed, hit play, and watch the black screen. I listen. "Start it over."

He hits play. "Crash. Have you, uh, seen my Walkman? I've been looking for it everywhere. I really need my beats."

Crash laughs a little. "Funny you should ask, Walkman. I saw it laying on the ground...at the park...and I wondered if it was yours. I'll get it to you tomorrow."

"I need it tonight. I mean, I listen to it to fall asleep and everything."

"Alright. Just give me a minute."

"Something's missing. My sta…my batteries. My batteries and tape are missing. Is this how you found it?"

Crash looks at me, eyes open wide, and points at the phone. "Did you hear the change?" I nod silently and put my fingers to my lips to shush him.

"Yes. It was… it was just lying there in the grass, and it was already open when I found it. Maybe some kids stole your tape and batteries, you know as a joke." There's an awkward silence. "Hey, man. Relax. Just tell me what tape it was and I'm sure I can get you another off Amazon. And the batteries...we can get some in the morning at the Dollar General. Don't you have another tape you can listen to that you like for a while?"

Walkman laughs nervously. His voice grows louder and more enunciated. "You don't get it, Crash. I'm not missing a tape and batteries. What I'm missing is something that belonged to someone else. I'm just... I'm just the runner. I drop, and I pick up. No questions asked. I get a cut, and they get the rest. It's how I pay the rent. It's how I pay for my grandma's reha. being in the hospital."

"Oh, shit."

"Yeah. You can say that again."

"You're a dealer. You deal drugs. You're a dealer."

"Stop repeating yourself, Crash. I'm not a dealer. I'm a runner. I drop the stash and pick up the cash. It's how I make money. But now I'm screwed. So unless you have a way to make a couple grand in two days, I suggest you keep your distance from me for a while." There's more silence. "What? Why are you starin' at me like that? I meant what I said! I've got bigger problems than you and your beer and your...buddies!"

"I'm sorry, man. You're just...you're just so different."

"All the world is a stage." Tom's voice just got quieter.

"I guess. You sure had me fooled with your happy-go-lucky attitude. I had no idea you were doin' what you're doin'."

Tom snorts in response. "I can't believe you never wondered how I pay my rent. It's not like I have a real job anywhere." He coughs. "I can't believe you took my headphones. I thought we were friends."

Crash snorts. "Are you friends with any of your other customers?"

"No." Tom talks to Crash like he's an idiot.

"Exactly." Crash mutters.

There's an awkward silence and then Crash is talking again. "What're you going to do, man? I mean, won't someone come for the money?"

There's a rustling sound and a pop tab being pulled. "It's one for the money, two for the show." I can't help but laugh. Tom's kind of a funny guy.

Another pause. "What the hell does that mean?"

Tom sounds annoyed. "I take it you're not an Elvis fan."

"What does Elvis have to do with any of this?" I can't help but grin at the annoyance in Crash's voice. He's not one for being patient.

"I don't know, but I've always wanted to hold my own court."

A few seconds go by. "I don't have an answer for that, but you're kind of up a creek without a paddle. Are you going to stick around for what comes next?"

"Where would I go? I know someone's coming, they always do! I don't know who it is... I don't want to know. They call me on my phone in a disguised voice. There are set drop off locations and times, and I have a routine. My routine's off, and they've already called my phone too many times today; I've just been ignoring it. I probably have two days tops before someone shows up. I'll just have to negotiate the loss."

"Don't get mad, but what if that doesn't work? I mean, what will they do if you don't have their money?" Crash almost sounds desperate.

"I don't know. This has never happened before. I've always been on time, and I've never had anything come up missing. Maybe The Neighbor will give me a break. He's always been somewhat decent. I mean, I don't know if he's in charge, but he's somewhere in the equation. Anyway, it's not your worry. Thanks for returning my player. Go on and take your beer. I need to be alone so I can think."

There's a pause. "Who's The Neighbor?" My brother sounds so clueless.

"I don't know!" Tom yells. A door slams.

The conversation ends. I feel Crash's eyes on me, but I stare hard at the floor, barely able to answer. "It's gone, Crash."

"What?"

"Whatever was in the tape player is gone. I threw it in the river."

He jumps up and stares down at me. "Why would you do that?"

I drop his phone on the bed, clench my fists, and look down at the floor. "I thought it was yours."

"You thought the drugs were mine?" Crash's voice is barely above a whisper.

I clap my hands over my ears and try to shut out his words. "Don't say that word, and yes, Crash, I thought it was yours. It was in your room in your bag. And you've been different lately. You're all moody. Half the time you're late to work, and you don't come home until early in the morning."

He plops down in the chair. "Ciara, I'm grieving, just like you. I just don't hide it as well."

All my feelings come spilling out as I glare at my idiotic brother. "Do you think you're the only one who's on the edge of falling apart? You know how much I wanted to just hide in my bed and never come out? I miss Mom and Dad too. So much. But they're gone, and all we can do is keep going and try to honor their memory."

Crash sneers up at me. "*Saint Ciara*. You do enough good for the two of us. You don't need to worry about me, I'll figure things out."

I glare back at him. "You dragged me into this, Crash. Now we're both stuck."

Crash crosses his arms on his chest. "Tom doesn't know what you did, and I'm not telling him."

I want to thank him, but that just feels wrong. "What about Denver?"

"What about him?"

"What does he know?"

Crash looks away, and I know what he's about to say is a lie. "Nothing."

I stare back at him. "Then why were the *both* of you in my room today?"

His face changes, and he looks on the verge of telling me the truth, but then he leans back. "You don't still have a crush on Denver, do you *little sister*?"

I blush just thinking about him. "No."

Crash smirks at me and I hate him so much right now. "That's good, because Denver and Gabi are very much together, if you know what I mean."

I know he says it because he's mad, but it still hurts. I glance over my dresser drawer and dread opening any texts I might get from Gabi. "Yeah, I know."

Crash pins me with a stare with his hand on the doorknob. "Ciara, you can't tell anyone about what you found."

I glare back at him. I'm pissed off beyond any coherent thought as I ground out. "Why would I want to?"

3

I go to school the next day, and pray it's my imagination, but I don't think so. I feel like I'm being watched as I walk up the school sidewalk. I glance around behind me, feeling all paranoid as I watch kids dart back and forth between the bus and the school. I want to shake the feeling as I head for my locker. *He* catches my eye, the one who lingers in the corners of my mind incessantly, despite my efforts to shove him out—Denver Evans. It's torture now that I know what a real kiss tastes like, what his skin feels like. He's way too obvious as he stares at me over Gabi's head. Quickly I shift my focus to Ari, Gabi, Magda, and Esmee who surround my locker.

I take a deep breath and pray they've forgotten about yesterday. "Hey, guys."

Gabi's eyes zero in on me like a tiger stalks its prey. "Hey, Ciara. What happened yesterday?"

Nothing much. I made out with your boyfriend and tossed some drugs in the river.

"Ciara!"

"What?"

"I asked you a question. What happened yesterday?"

I shrug my shoulders. "Nothing too exciting."

"You dropped our FaceTime call."

"I did? I guess my phone battery died."

Gabi's eyes narrow, and she eyes me hard. "Really? The whole night?"

I look away, uncomfortable and fumbling. "Well, you know, I had some reading to do for English."

Ari high fives me. "Get it, girl."

I nod my head, thankful for the reprieve from Gabi's twenty questions. "Yep."

I open my locker. I'm startled to see a small box sitting on the top shelf. Something about it feels secretive. I turn away, sneak it in my backpack, and head to first hour, sliding into the back row. I'm thoroughly irritated when Denver walks past me and nudges my foot with his before plopping into the chair beside me, scooting his whole desk sideways. What is going on?

No sooner does class start than I excuse myself, take my bag and run to the girl's restroom. I step into the stall and make sure no one else is around. I dig out the box and shake it but hear no sound.

I pry the top off and pull out a bunch of bubble tape. There's a SD card in the middle. What in the world? I shove it all back in, feeling panicky, thinking someone definitely made a mistake, when I see the initials on the bottom of the box. "C.O.Y." is written in small, little black lettering. I sit down before my knees give out, and that's when I see the square slip of white paper on the floor. I lean over, pick it up, and flip it over.

RULES OF SURVIVAL

1. Never forget the game
2. Curiosity kills more than cats
3. The Neighbor is always watching
4. Snitches get Stitches

My stomach turns over, and I think I might puke, but there's another part of me that's been awakened; an excitement I want to squash and ignore, the part that can't wait to see what's on the SD card. In the back of my mind, I know who put the box in my locker, just like I know who was watching me walk into school. My mind slowly stutter-steps backwards; if Denver was inside waiting for me to find the box, he couldn't have been outside. I slip the paper in my pocket and the box back in my bag. Unease fills me. Who followed me to school today?

The rest of the day passes in a blur, and I can't think of anything but getting home to see what is on the SD card. Finally, the last bell rings, and I fly out of the school. I'm sitting at my laptop, ready to pop in the card, when I get a Snapchat from Char. "Aren't you supposed to be at Spanish club?"

I answer her quickly. "Not feelin' it."

"I didn't feel like going to work today but I went anyway." I ignore her scathing remark. "Hello?"

"Chill, Char. It's the first week of school." I shove my phone back in my dresser drawer.

I shove the SD card in, open the video, and completely ignore the warning I just received about curiosity.

An old woman lies in bed in a dark room. She's so still, she looks dead. I think I hear a door opening off-screen. Someone walks in and comes close to her bedside, but their back is to the camera. Her eyes fly open. She whips her bony neck around sideways to wave a skeletal hand at them. "Get out of here! Leave me alone! Let an old woman rest in peace!"

"Ms. Wood, I'm here to take your vitals." It's a woman's voice.

"I said get out! My doctor is the only person who's allowed in here. Now go!"

As if summoned, there's a knock at the door. "What are you doing in my patient's room?" The demanding voice is offscreen. The man's voice is quiet but commanding.

"I'm sorry, Doctor. I was just doing my rounds." I giggle to myself. The nurse doesn't sound a bit sorry.

"This woman is my patient, and I gave strict orders for no one to come in here. She has an unknown virus. It could be contagious."

"Then where is your PPE, Doctor?" I like this sassy nurse.

"Excuse me, what?" the doctor asks.

The nurse sighs. "PPE—personal, protective, equipment?"

"Don't tell me how to treat my patient! Just get out! And don't come in here again!" There's a pause. "And shut that door behind you. It's never to be opened!"

"But sir, what about her meals?"

"Call me Doctor, and I will take care of her meals. Keep the damn door shut!"

There's a sound of the door closing. The doctor approaches the bedside, finally stepping into the picture, but all I see is his back. "Playing chess again, are we?"

The woman lies in her bed. She pulls something out from beneath the covers, lifts an unlit cigarette to dangle from her lips, and gives him a creepy smile. "I enjoy a good strategy."

"Pondering your next move?"

She turns her head toward the windows. "Some things cannot be rushed. For everything there is a season, and the smell of the harvest is not yet in the air."

He sighs. "You know I hate it when you speak in riddles."

She looks back at him. "I lie here day after day in the dark. The cold seeps through my bones as I hide from the sunlight hovering behind the curtain's edge." She points toward the windows. "My memory is my only company; how I long for the days of windy car rides and bare feet running on hot pavement that fly off the never-ending slide show emerging to mute the background of these long empty hallways and demented prisoners."

He chuckles. "You do love your drama, I'll give you that."

She laughs creepily. "Yes. For now, I rest in quiet solitude, keeping my words and thoughts trapped inside. My silence and snarling disposition wards off any who dare approach."

He moves to the base of her bed and taps her foot. "Sounds like you've got it all under control."

She jerks her foot away, hissing. "Don't touch me."

He sits at down at the end of her bed, still turned away from the camera. "There was a time..."

She cackles. "Those days are long gone. Let's focus on the game, shall we?"

He stands up, crosses his arms. It's maddening. His back is still to the camera. "Ah, yes. The game. It seems the boy is in a bit of trouble."

"Oh?"

"Yes. He lost his product, or so he says." My stomach drops.

The woman shifts in her bed, taps her fingers on the blanket, and gazes off again. "Just remember. The King with the most pawns always wins in the end."

The man clears his throat. "Yes, well. It takes a steady, cautious hand to keep all the pawns on the board, and positioning the pawns is second nature for the practiced hand of a master manipulator."

She stares up at him. "It takes all the pawns for the game play out." Seconds pass as they stare at each other. "See you later, Doctor, you're dismissed."

The man stands up, walks closer to the woman, and stares down at her for a few minutes as she continues to look away from him, gazing out the window. He slowly but surely turns over all her chess pieces, and still, she ignores him as he leans closer to her bed. "Let the games begin." He mutters just above a whisper before he walks away. There's the sound of a door shutting.

The woman turns back to face the camera. The rage on her face fills my laptop screen, and I shudder and move instinctively away from the screen. She grabs a chess piece and chucks it out of sight. A loud crash is heard offscreen. She throws her head back and screams at the top of her lungs with her arms outstretched. The veins in her neck strain. I'm sure I'll have nightmares tonight.

I watch the screen for the next 30 minutes, but nothing happens, and I can't stand to watch the creepy old woman with flowing white hair stare out the window at nothing any longer. I leave the SD card going as I get out my homework. I'm in for a long night, as I couldn't seem to focus on anything today. I'm on my fourth hour of homework, feeling pretty good, when I hear a noise. I flip back over to the SD card video. The room is pitch black, but there's the sound of the door opening. Quick footsteps cross the floor. There's a rustling of the bed sheets. Is there someone in there with her? What are they doing? My heart races as I wait for more, but there's just silence.

About twenty minutes later, there's footsteps again, and a rustling sound. The sound of something hits the floor. More footsteps. More silence. This happens about three times, and I have no idea what is going on. It's most infuriating, and it feels too much like watching *The Blair Witch Project*. I get back to my homework and finish up. I glance at my school e-mail and see I have a message from an unknown address, subject matter COY. I click on it.

"Did you get the package?"

I can't believe I answer. "Watching now."

I'm startled by the swift reply. "Return package to its original spot."

I try to confirm the sender's identity. "Is this another secret?"

There's another reply. "S N I T C H E S G E T S T I T C H E S."

I close the e-mail with trembling fingers.

I'm about ready to turn off the video when I hear voices again. The doctor's back. I turn back over to the video, and I'm puzzled that they're talking in the dark. I glance at the time onscreen. It's 1:30 in the morning! What doctor visits their patient at 1:30 a.m.?

"My reputation is at stake."

There's a coughing spell followed by laughter. "What reputation? You're a nobody."

"I'll show him I'm no one to be trifled with."

"He's not worth your time."

"I can't afford to be soft, not on any level." The doctor answers.

"Words make you soft. You don't have the stomach for painting." Why does her hard voice sound soft and cajoling?

"Jimmy does. I never minded watching. I just don't want paint on my hands. You can't wash the soul."

She laughs. "Since when did you get religious on me?"

"I like to keep my options open."

More laughter ensues. "Whatever you say. Give him a little more time. Money's always better than murder, and training someone new takes time." Murder?

"It's more than a small loss... there was a mistake."

"Oh? What kind of mistake?" Why does she sound so excited?

"A brick was switched."

"And?"

"There's a significant difference in value."

"So the brick that was lost is more valuable."

"Yes. And it makes me wonder if it was really lost or if he caught the mistake and profited from it."

"That's a very serious assumption, and if the mistake was yours... why should he pay for it?"

"There's someone above me, and they want the value of what was lost." The doctor sounds desperate. This is not good.

"Do you need a loan?"

The man clears his throat. "I'll pay you back."

"Come back tomorrow in the evening. I'll have it then."

"Thank you. This is just between us, right?"

"Of course. Watch your step with Jimmy. He's a bulldog. He's got a vicious bite."

"That *is* the point."

"And you trust him?"

"As much as I trust you." There are more footsteps and then a door closes.

"That's your first mistake." She whispers into the darkness. Her voice curdles my blood, and I shudder again. The old lady is nuts, and she belongs in a psyche ward, but she's also scary as hell, and I hope I never meet her. My mind runs in circles the rest of the night. Who is this woman and who is the man? I'm not sure I'd recognize him if I can't see his face. More importantly—who sent me the video and why?

4

I wake up all ready to go to school. I grab a pop tart on my way out the door. The small box weighs heavy in the bottom of my backpack.

"Where are you going?" I almost fall over as Crash's voice catches me off guard as I step off the porch.

I sigh. "To school."

He laughs. "Nope. It's Fishing Derby Day."

"What? No, it's Friday."

"Ciara. How could you forget Fishing Derby Day? It's our tradition." I race back inside, look at the calendar, and blink twice when I see that it is Friday, but there's no school today. I run back upstairs, shove my backpack clear in a corner, grab a hat, my phone, and some sunscreen. I race back down the stairs and poke my head out the front door.

"You have our lunches?"

"Check."

"Waters?"

"Check."

"Poles?"

"Ciara! Come on. If we don't go, we might not get our spot."

"Fine. Race you to the truck!"

I take off down the front steps, but Crash clears the porch railing, cuts across the driveway, and grins as he lands in the front seat, out of breath. I laugh and climb up in the truck.

He turns the key in the ignition. "Man, do I need today."

We start down the road. He stops at the corner, and I see Denver running toward us. "Crash. What are we doing?"

He coughs. "Denver's never been to the fishing derby. He asked if he could go."

"I don't think..."

Denver yanks open the door and grins at me. My insides turn to mush. "Hey, guys! Got room for one more?"

I look down at Denver from the truck, thinking it'd be best if I just walked home; but instead, I scoot over next to Crash to give him room. "Sure."

Crash shoves me sideways, knocking me into Denver. He gives me his ornery brotherly grin as he chews on his toothpick. "Shove off, Ciara. Don't sit so close."

Embarrassed, I scoot over toward Denver, who throws his arm around me and gives my shoulder a squeeze. "Who's ready to go fishing?"

Crash punches the gas and squeals his tires. "Here we go."

We tear down the road to the lake, and it feels like Crash hits every pothole along the way, bumping me so hard I almost land in Denver's lap. Denver glances over at him. "Trying to break an axle, Crash?"

My brother just laughs. "This old Ford can handle it."

I breathe a sigh of relief when we get to the Derby. Soon enough, we're walking clear around the lake. With my folding lawn chairs in hand and backpack over my shoulder, I can't wait for a day of relaxation. Who am I kidding? That SD card is going to run through my brain like a computer programming loop.

We get to our favorite spot, a little beach area with a natural hidden cove. I plop down in my chair, dig out a novel, and fold my feet into the chair. I relax with my pole propped up in a cement brick on the ground in front of me.

Denver glances over at Crash and then me. "You two gonna sit here in silence all day?"

I smile and look over at Crash, waiting for Dad's words of wisdom. He gives me a wink as he answers Denver. "The trick is in the stillness. You gotta be patient and immovable; unnoticeable." My throat tightens as I hear Dad's tone in Crash's voice.

Denver moseys over to me, shaking his head. "If you say so. Ciara, you got another book in there?"

I blush at the thought, as I'm pretty sure all I've got in my bag are romance novels. They're my vacation reading. I look up at him and take a breath. "I've got what I've got. Take it or leave it."

I pull three out and hand them to him. He raises his eyebrows at the covers and smiles down at me. "Tough choice." He snatches one up. "I think I'll take 'Lady in Waiting'." I can't help but laugh as I put my books away.

Crash snorts. "Denver, are you really going to read that nonsense?"

Denver hits Crash with the book. "If you're not going to talk to me, yeah."

The afternoon passes in a comfortable silence, and I almost forget Denver is here until lunch time. We unpack the cooler, and I make the sandwiches before handing them out. Crash digs out the pop and I unpack the graham cracker frosting sandwiches, my favorite. Denver grins like a little boy. "You go all out."

Crash laughs while he stands at the water's edge with his sandwich. He skips rocks on the water. "Just wait 'til you have a brownie. Ciara makes the best brownies."

Denver looks over at me, and I'm back in the kitchen with him, as his fingers flirt with mine when we reach for the graham crackers. "I just bet she does." I choke a little on my pop, look away, and try to find a way to ask Denver something without being obvious, but I can't, and I'm feeling pretty desperate.

"Hey, did you find anything unexpected in your locker?"

His face remains clueless as he chuckles. "Like what?"

I feel stupid. "Nothing. Just never mind."

He squeezes my pinkie. "Ciara, are you okay?"

Two can play this game, as I look him in the eye. "Never better." I quickly pack up the lunches and put everything away. We settle in for the afternoon. Time flies as I finish reading my novel and reach into my bag for another. I glance at my watch. It's about 4:00 p.m. "Apples and cheese time."

Denver smiles over at me. "I've got to hang out with you two more often. You really know how to eat."

I giggle and unpack the Braeburn apples, French bread, and cheddar cheese cubes. We all grab a water. We munch on our snacks before I toss my breadcrumbs in the lake, watching as the turtles and fish swim to the surface.

Denver takes off running. "I gotta take a leak."

I blush and turn away, catching Crash's movements, so quick and smooth, I almost miss the worry that skitters across his face as he glances up the hill. I follow his gaze. I'm surprised to see Walkman coming down through the grass. He walks so deliberate, straight, and true with none of his signature careless and free bouncing step. He looks like a stranger. Crash was right about his strange transformation; I almost can't believe it.

Two men follow in the distance. Crash grabs my arm and spins me around. "Don't look at them." I fight him and try to turn back around, but he grips my arm tightly. "Ciara, you've got to go now, before they see you. It's better if you don't see them. You don't want to be a witness."

My heart freezes for a second in terror, and I can't catch my breath. "Witness to what? What are you saying, Crash?" My voice is too loud, but I can't help it.

Crash squeezes my arm hard. "Ciara, shut up. I'm sure I'll be fine. I'm saying you can't snitch if you don't know who they are. Please, just go." I'm terrified at the fear I hear in his voice. This is my big brother. He's not afraid of anything.

I whisper back to him. "Where am I going to go, Crash? We're halfway around the lake."

His eyes dart around as his grip on my arm grows tighter. "Walk the lakeshore around the bend and stay there until I come find you. You've got to go now! Hurry!"

I hate deserting my brother, but I have no choice. I run away from Crash, stooping low as I go, trying to stay below the riverbank, sneaking around the corner, praying no one's on the other side. Luckily, the lake shore is bare. I see no one near before I scan the opposite shoreline. I spy kids from my school in a group across the lake. They wave and call out to me. I wave back and quickly turn away, as if to cue them to be quiet. It's a strange sensation to be scared to death and yet play-act like nothing is wrong. I want desperately to call for help; but between the list of rules and the weird video, I'm petrified. I don't know what Tom and the men are up to with Crash, but it can't be good. I try to calm down. Surely, they won't do anything too terrible in broad daylight at a fishing derby.

I lay flat on the sand and scoot as close as I can to the other side of the wall. As I hug the other side of the cove, I see a small hole. I peek through it to spy on them, but the sound goes away; so I put my ear up to the hole, straining.

Someone clears their throat. "Hey, Crash. I thought you might be out here. I, um, was telling the guys how you found my player and returned it to me…empty."

"We've already had this conversation, Walkman, which is why I'm not sure why you're here. You know when I found it, it was lying empty on the ground." I cringe at the anger in my brother's tone.

"Hold up there, Jimmy. No need to do anything rash. We came here to talk, remember?" Oh, no. It's the guy from the video! I recognize his voice.

Someone grunts.

The other voice continues. "Crash, this equation isn't hard to solve. Walkman took my product. He owes me money. He says you took the container holding the product. I just want my cut. That's all."

"And how much would that cut be, exactly?" I wish my brother would cool down.

"Three grand."

"Three grand! It's always been fifteen hundred," Tom's voice whines.

"Being that I've had to take time out of my busy schedule to come down here, and your drop was late, the price is double. You've got a week to get it to me."

"I don't have that kind of cash." My brother's telling the truth, and I hope they believe him.

There's silence, and I look through the hole. The man seems to be glancing at the short stocky man who stands closest to my brother. The taller, thin man gives the stocky guy a small nod. How I wish he would turn around. In seconds, the short man is on Crash. He whips a gun from behind his back and spins Crash around toward the water, knocking him in the back of the head, stunning him. I clap my hand over my mouth as I watch in frozen terror. The man drags my brother to the water's edge like Crash is some kind of featherweight and shoves his head in. He holds him under for an eternity, yanking him out long enough for Crash to take a breath, and he's under again. He does this at least four times before his partner calls him off. "That's enough, Jimmy." He growls.

Jimmy's already got his head under again. "That's enough I said!" Jimmy yanks Crash up and flops him on to his back like a rag doll. His lower half is still in the water. His back is in the sand. The short man shoulder bumps Walkman as he heads out of sight with a terrifying smirk on his face.

Walkman's face goes white as a sheet when Jimmy leans in and whispers something to him.

The tall man walks toward Crash. He stops when he's standing directly over him, as Crash lies on the shore, gasping for air. "I didn't ask if you had it. You're going to get it for me. One week. Let's go, Tom."

Crash lies helpless and unmoving, watching the men walk back up over the hill. My vision goes blurry as tears fill my eyes. I watch my brother as his breathing slows. I fight hyperventilation. I want to run to him, but I can't. What if the men see me? If I know Crash like I do, it won't be long before his anger will kick in and revive him, but right now his whole body trembles from the aftershock of the attack. He stares up at the sky, and I wonder what he's thinking. I rub my arms vigorously, fighting goosebumps of fear.

I breathe deeply and watch my brother, trying to decide when it's safe to come out. I can't stop blinking. Did all of that really just happen right in front of me? I feel like I'm in a mobster movie. I'm so mad at Tom right now, I could strangle him with my bare hands.

There's movement as Crash rolls over to his front and pushes himself up off the ground. He crawls a small distance, coughing up water as he goes. Struggling, he makes it to his feet. He stumbles around the bend on wobbly legs that look like limp spaghetti. He tries to look all casual, but I know better, and he must see it on my face as my voice comes out in a hoarse whisper. "Crash. What are we going to do? Those men. They can't come back. You seeing them again isn't an option."

Crash rubs the back of his neck, stares at the ground, and kicks the rocks into the lake. "This isn't your concern, Ciara. You had nothing to do with this."

I chew on my lip, a nervous habit I can't seem to break. "Crash! What do you mean? I had *everything* to do with this! I'm the reason they were here today!"

Crash slams his hand into his leg. "No, Ciara! If I hadn't stolen the player, you wouldn't have thought I was doin' drugs, and you wouldn't have found what you did in my room."

I try not to sound judgmental. "*Why* was it in your room?"

He coughs. "It was just a stupid joke, okay? I was at the park with my friends, playing disc golf, and Tom was sleeping on a park bench. You know how the guys can be; one of them dared someone to steal his Walkman, but no one would, so I did, and now I wish I would have just left him alone."

I pull out one of his leg hairs, I'm so mad. "No kidding, Crash. I can't believe this huge mess started from a dare at the park." But really, I'm blaming it on Denver, because if he hadn't kissed me in my room, I wouldn't have gone to Crash's room, and if I hadn't gone there, we wouldn't be here, but of course, I can't say any of that. I clear my throat. "Well. We both did something stupid. But really, this is Tom's fault. He doesn't have to be a runner."

Crash looks at me. He gets all defensive. "Tom's got his own problems and his own reasons."

After everything that just happened, I can't believe my stupid brother! "Crash!" The harshness in my voice scares the both of us as my brother leans away from me, but I'm fired up. My voice comes out low and filled with venom. "I can't believe you're defending Tom! He's practically a drug dealer! He led those men right to you! He almost got you killed just now! Open your eyes! We *all* have choices! Tom *made* his! You shouldn't have to pay for his stupidity!"

Crash looks back at me like I slapped him, and I wish I had. He whispers furiously back. "Keep your voice down, Ciara! You don't know who's listening. Tom's just trying to take care of his mom and pay his rent. Anyway, like it or not, Ciara, we're in it now, and there's no getting out. Those men aren't gonna just go away. We need to come up with a plan."

I focus on breathing as I stare off into the distance and try to cool off. I'm so mad at my brother I can't look at him. "You want *me* to figure out how to outrun two dealers, save *your* butt, but *not* call the cops?"

Crash huffs. "And tell them what? That I *accidentally* stole some drugs and then you threw them in the river? Do you honestly think they'll believe us?"

I dig my fingernails into my palms. "It might be worth a shot; but if you say no, I'll wait. For now. But I've already decided I'm not telling Charlotte any of this. She has enough to worry about."

Crash laughs. "Trust me. I'm not telling her a thing. That's all I need is her yelling at me. Come on, let's go get our stuff. I've had enough of the lake today." Crash muses. "I know I've seen that man before, but where?"

I purse my lips together and keep silent. I know where I've heard his voice, but I'm not saying a word.

We walk around the bend to find Denver packing everything up. I can't help but wonder at his perfect timing. How is it that he *missed* my brother being threatened, half drowned, and walked right back in just as they exited?

Denver looks over at me. "Everything okay?"

I study him for a minute before answering. "Why don't you ask Crash?"

5

The ride home is a tense one. I sit beside Denver, not wanting to touch him, but not wanting to be next to my brother, either. I wrack my brain, trying to come up with an escape plan, when I hear my chemistry teacher's words in my ears. "When you're trying to solve a problem, think of something else and it'll come to you." I start thinking about the novel we're reading in English class, and then I remember our vocab quizzes and the closet of flea market treasures/prizes, and that's when it hits me. "Dummy!"

Crash turns to me. "Excuse me?"

I clear my throat in embarrassment. "Nothing."

Crash drops off Denver, who hops out of the truck and gives me a funny look. "See you later, Ciara."

I say nothing as I wave at him in dismissal.

We pull away and head toward our house.

Crash glances over at me. "What's up with you two? Lover's quarrel?"

I look back at him. "You *do know* he's dating Gabi, right?"

He laughs. "That doesn't mean anything."

I glare at him. "Whatever. Don't you think it's just a little *convenient* Denver was gone the entire time those guys were with you."

"What do you mean?"

How can Crash not figure this out? "I'm just saying. His timing couldn't have been more perfect."

"You really think that Denver knows them, and that he's somehow part of this?"

I remember the slip of paper again. "I don't know what I think, Crash. I'm probably just being paranoid. I'm feeling beat right now."

"Ciara, are you going to help me?" The helpless desperation in his voice annoys me because I can't ignore it.

"Yes, Crash, but I'm tired. Tomorrow's Saturday. I'll have all day to come up with something."

He nods his head. "True. Good idea. Get some rest."

I rush upstairs and check my closet for my bag and the box at the bottom.

I perch on the windowsill and stare down at the driveway as I try to form a plan in my mind. I'm halfway through it when my thoughts are interrupted by Tom and the stocky guy backing Crash's truck out of our driveway. I slip off the ledge and duck down to take a few pics by holding up my phone while I crouch beneath the curtain in case anyone's looking up. Seconds later, I tear down the stairs, run out the back door, and head for my brother's apartment. "Crash! They took your truck!"

"I must've left my keys in it." He mumbles through a closed door.

He steps out of the bathroom in nothing but a towel. I wheel around, embarrassed. "Gross. At least warn me next time."

He chuckles. "You're in *my* apartment, Ciara. Who took my truck?"

"Tom and the lake guy! Aren't you going to call the police?"

He pounds his fist on the countertop. "I can't call the police! I'm not exactly innocent. We'll just have to wait 'til they come back."

He comes around in his jeans, tugging his shirt on. "Do you have a plan yet?"

It hits me. "We have to make it look like you're gone."

"For how long do you think? What about my job? I can't just quit."

I take a deep breath. "No, Crash. Like permanently gone."

His eyes start to bug. "You want to kill me?"

I slap his leg. "Not for real, idiot. It just has to look like you died, and they have to see it."

He looks at me like I'm nuts, and I think I might be. "Are you out of your damn mind, Ciara?"

"It's the only way, Crash. They're never going to leave you alone otherwise."

"I don't know. That seems a bit extreme."

"And you think being half-drowned isn't? He could've killed you." My voice gets quieter the more scared I get, and by the time I finish my sentence, I'm whispering.

He swallows hard. "Okay, I'll do it, but Ciara sometimes you scare me."

I look down at my hands in my lap. "I know the feeling."

"What?"

I jerk my head up and stare at the side of his face. I'm still annoyed with him and the mess we're in. "Someone's got to come up with an idea, and you certainly aren't."

He sighs. "No need to be rude."

I clear my throat. "We're going to need help, but it has to be someone we can trust."

"Walkman?"

"No."

"Denver?"

"I... I don't know. I'm still working on it."

We sit down on opposite ends of the couch, and he turns on *Friends*, but it's just background noise.

After a while, he glances at his watch and heads for the door. "They've been gone forty-five minutes. I don't like this. I've got a really bad feeling."

As much as I hate it, I agree, and I can't stay here. "I'm going with you." My eyes widen as Crash reaches up in the closet by the door and pulls out a pistol. "Where'd you get that?"

His eyes water a little as he stares at me. "It was Dad's."

"Oh." I follow my brother to our shared car, feeling like an alien as I watch him shove the pistol in the waist of his jeans as we go down the stairs. I put on a seatbelt, and we start down the road that heads out of town. My eyes struggle to focus. I grab the door handle as he whips down a side road. "Crash!"

"I think I just saw Tom." He mutters as he keeps his eyes on the road.

He races down the dirt road. Gravel flies everywhere, and I pray we don't get a flat, as he slams on the brakes, and we almost fishtail off the road. He slams it into park, jumps out of the car, and yells at me. "Ciara! Get the tarp out of the trunk and throw it on the backseat!"

I do as I'm told, running around the driver side to pull the lever to the trunk, yanking the tarp out, laying it out as fast as I can. I turn to see my brother drag a limp Tom out of the ditch and somehow manage to get him in the car. His shirt is covered in blood. I run back around to shut the trunk. Crash is on the other side, leaning over Tom, who dangles out one side of the car. Crash grabs Tom's pant loops. "Ciara, get his legs inside the car. Push when I say pull."

"Get your junk out of my face, Crash." Tom mutters.

Crash stares down at him. "Shut up and save your energy, Tom. We're going to the hospital." Crash looks over at me. "Ready?" I nod. "One, two, three, push" I push on Tom's knees as Crash pulls on his waist, and we manage to get all of Tom in the car. I shut the door. Crash does the same. We hop in the front.

Tom's talking. "I got him, Crash. I shot Jimmy the Bulldog." He laughs in between moans. "He shot me first, but I had the last word." He rolls over, moaning. "Damn, this hurts like a son of a bitch."

I glance down at Tom and wonder how I could be so angry at a man who might be dying in my backseat; but I am. "Where's our truck?"

Tom smiles at me. "Up shit creek." He laughs again.

I glare at him. "No more jokes, Tom."

His eyes stop dancing, and he talks between breaths. "It's halfway down the creek bed. In the water. Jimmy gave me no choice. They were going to take me out to pasture." He looks at me. "Like a cow, Ciara. They were going to shoot me like a cow in a pasture. Like an animal."

I can't look at him anymore, so I turn back around.

We pull up to Cary's garage, and I turn to Crash. "What are you doing?"

"I'm giving him to Cary to take him to the station. The nearest hospital is twenty miles from here. I don't know if he'll make it that far."

Tom speaks up from the back seat in between ragged breaths. "Go to the pay phone on 3rd. Call 911. Lay me out on the ground and wait around the corner to be sure the EMTs find me."

Crash backs out of Cary's driveway and we do exactly what Tom says. Soon enough, the ambulance arrives. Crash and me duck down as they load up Tom. As soon as they're gone, we head back down the road to the creek bed.

I race after Crash as he runs down the steep embankment, and we head around the corner together. I spy his truck a ways away and point it out. Crash turns to me. "He wasn't kidding."

I look at him. "How are we going to get your truck out of the water?"

Crash runs over to it and opens the door. I hold in a gasp at the sight of the man's empty eyes. It's hard to believe he was holding my brother underwater not that long ago. Crash swallows hard as he side-eyes me. "I can't believe Tom shot him." He white knuckles the truck door. "We've got bigger problems than moving my truck." He reaches in, snatches something, and sticks it in his pocket.

I hear a cough from across the water. I duck down behind the back truck wheel. Crash reaches for his pistol as he ducks down beside me. "Relax you two, it's just me."

I breathe a sigh of relief as I stand up to face Cary, my sister's on-and-off again boyfriend. "Hey, Cary."

He frowns at us. "You two don't seem too shocked to see a dead body in the truck."

Crash looks back at him. "How long have you been here, Cary, and how do you know what's in there? I didn't know you could see anything from over there."

Cary wades through the creek bed in his tall rubber boots. "I heard on the scanner there was a body in a truck, so I came on down to investigate."

"So you're an official deputy now?"

"Not exactly, Crash, but you know the county is short-handed." He walks over, takes out his phone, and snaps a few pictures.

Crash looks at him. "I want it on your records what time we got here."

Cary studies him. "Fine. You want to tell me what you know?"

Crash crosses his arms on his chest. "I know someone stole my truck and took it down a creek bed."

Cary looks over at him. "Do you know the man in the truck?"

Crash shakes his head. "No."

Cary narrows his eyes. "So you had no idea he was a hitman?"

I cough, and Crash rocks back on his heels, and squeezes the top of his nose as if he feels a nosebleed coming on. "No, I didn't."

I know it's not wise, but I have to ask. "How *big* of a hitman?"

Cary gives me a funny look. "Does it matter?"

I stare back at him, surprised at my answer. "Yeah, it matters. How do we know a bunch of guys won't come looking for the person who shot him?"

Cary throws up his hands. "We don't, but right now that's the least of my worries."

Crash looks back at Cary. "When can I get my truck back?"

Cary looks at Crash like he's crazy. "I don't know, Crash. It's evidence now. There's a dead body. They're going to have to dust it for fingerprints and analyze the crime scene."

I plop down on a log and try to process everything. "How long do we have to stay?"

Cary looks back at me. "I guess you two can go. I know where to find you if I have questions."

Crash gives him a salute. "Later, Cary."

I follow my brother up the riverbank and we walk to the car. Crash drives slow on the way home. Right before we get to the main road, the sheriff flies by with lights and sirens going. I glance over at Crash, who stares straight ahead. "Why was Cary there? I mean, don't you think it was weird how fast he got there?"

"You heard him, Ciara. He's helping out because they're short-staffed." He sounds all irritated, and I should probably keep quiet, but my mind can't slow down.

"This is serious, Crash. It's a *murder scene*."

He stares at me for a second. "You don't think I know that?"

"I'm just saying, where are the detectives if it's a murder scene? They have to have special people. I saw it on T.V."

"Well, this isn't T.V., Ciara. We live in a small town with no money for special agents and detectives. Not everything in life is like the movies."

I shake my head and consider the secret package in my locker, the woman in the video, the fact that my brother was almost drowned by a hitman, and that I'm about to stage a hanging. "Are you sure about that, Crash?"

He slaps the steering wheel. "Ciara! Stop talking! I can't take any more of your smart mouth right now."

I wiggle in my seat and bite my tongue for a few seconds, but that's as long as I can stand it. "I just think it's weird how Cary's so close to the police department."

He jerks his head sideways. "I don't know, Ciara. I don't have all the answers. All I know is if Cary's on our side, and he's in with the police department, well, that's not all bad."

I sit here thinking. "You're right about that, but I think Cary knows something about everything that's been going on. He didn't seem too surprised about the body in your truck, either, and I think it's strange he just showed up out of the blue. I mean, you didn't call him, did you?"

"I just mentioned the scanner, twice! And like I said, we don't talk much anymore."

An idea comes to me. "Wait. Are you on Snapchat with Cary?"

"Yeah. Why?"

"I bet he can see your location on his phone. I mean, it'd be pretty easy for him to track you through Snapchat is all."

"Oh, I didn't think of that. But does it work that great out in the boonies? I mean, we were down in a creek-bed."

"I think so. I mean, it works well enough. It's just as well he found you. Pulling a dead body out of your truck would not have been the smartest thing to do."

"Whatever, Ciara. You threw drugs in the river! I was just trying to think of how to get my truck back. I never said I was going to move the body, but what's it matter where he died? He's still dead."

I shiver when I think of a man dying in my brother's truck. "What was on the note?"

Crash's face looks blank as he looks back at me. "What note?"

I hate it when he plays all ignorant. "Don't play dumb with me, Crandall. I saw you stick something in your pocket."

"You know I hate that name." He digs the folded up note out of his pocket and hands it to me. "For all I know, the note could have been for Jimmy, the dead guy."

My voice trembles. "But what if it's for you? What if Tom's partner found Jimmy first and left this note for you? We have to have a plan. And we have to do it fast. I mean, there's no way you'll come up with three thousand by this Saturday, and who knows what the partner will do now that Tom killed Jimmy."

We're home now and parked in the driveway. Crash turns to yell at me. "I know, Ciara, okay? I know! But I kind of owe Tom. He tried to protect me by getting rid of Jimmy!"

I have to make him see reason. "Crash! We both heard Tom. It was self-preservation that made him shoot Jimmy! That's all."

He glares at me. "Ciara, just read the damn note."

I pick up the piece of folded paper. I don't want to see what's inside. I lay it back down on the seat between us as I unfold it. I wish I'd never touched it as I see the scrawled letters in bold, black writing. *"You're next."*

6

I sit in the kitchen in view of the back-porch screen door, munching on almonds and carrots, watching to be sure Crash is in his apartment, waiting for Cary to return. Once I see his headlights, I run to the garage and pull out my bicycle. I'm thankful Cary's garage is at the end of our sidewalk block. I get there quickly and stow my bike behind a pile of tires outside as I sneak in the side door.

I knock on the doorframe as I enter. I spy Cary's long legs sticking out from beneath his silver dreamboat car with black racing stripes down the side. "Hey, Cary."

He leans out from underneath the door. "What's up, small Yengst?"

I used to hate the nickname, but I've come to love it, because not every guy makes me feel delicate. I plop down on a stack of tires and sink in the middle as my legs hang over the edges. He laughs. "Careful. You might get treadmarks on your ass."

I throw my hands up. "Guess it's good I'm wearing black shorts."

"What's on your mind?"

My mind races, and I don't know how much to tell him, but I need help. "I, ah, I need your help with something, and I can't tell Char."

"Oh?"

"Yeah. It has to do with the truck in the creek bed. Crash is kind of in trouble, and I'm kind of the reason." I hate that my voice wavers. I don't want to cry in front of Cary. I take a deep breath. The silence is deafening. "I, um, I have a plan. I just need some help carrying it out is all."

"And you think that I'm going to be on board with this?"

I sigh. "You haven't even heard the plan yet." I take another deep breath. "It's kind of out there. Well, it's really out there, but it's the only way to keep Crash safe and to keep my family safe. I've messed up, Cary. It's bad. And I've got to make it right."

He peeks out at me again. I look at him upside down. My view fits my life. "What's your plan?"

"We're going to fake Crash's death to buy us some time." I can't believe I said this out loud.

"What? How are you going to do that?"

"I'm going to stage a hanging in the old barn past the river."

"Why there?"

"It's abandoned and no one goes out there. It's hidden in the woods."

"What do you need me to do?"

"I can't get this done with just Crash, and you're the mechanic. I thought you could help us rig it up."

"So Crash knows about this, and he's okay with it?"

I kick my shoes against the pile of tires. "Crash told me to come up with a plan, so I did. He had no idea what to do."

Cary studies me. "There's more going on in that mind of yours than I like to think about."

I stick out my tongue. "Whatever, *weed boy.*"

He frowns. "That was a long time ago. I'm done with that. I've been reformed. I'm just waiting for your sister to believe in me."

I look down at him. His face is all sincere, but this is my sister. "She could do so much better than you, you know."

He grunts. "Thanks for your vote of confidence."

I giggle. "I never said I didn't like you. Don't give up."

He winks. "Thanks. I won't."

We sit here a while longer, and I can't help but admire his beautiful car. "So, you ever going to take her out on the track?"

He drops a wrench on the floor. "*She* is a *He*, and maybe. I don't know, though. I'd hate to mess up his gorgeous paint job."

I wiggle out of the tires until my toes touch the floor. "See you later, Cary."

"Bye, small Yengst."

I turn back. "Don't you want to know what sort of mess I'm in?"

He sticks his head out from underneath the car. "No. The less I know the better." He ducks back under and out of sight.

I stand here, feeling uncertain, wishing he would ask for more information. It's a lot for me to handle all by myself. A few seconds go by, and there's no more movement. "Thanks, Cary."

"You're welcome." I've been dismissed.

I walk outside and reach for my bike. A hand grabs mine from out of the darkness, pulling me in. I hold in my scream and follow Denver's scent. We stop at the back corner of Cary's garage. His shoulder touches mine as he leans in to whisper. "What are you doing here?"

I turn to answer him. Our faces are so close, my lips almost brush his shoulder. "I'm talking to Cary."

"About what?"

The words are on the tip of my tongue, but I remember the SD card and Denver's faked cluelessness. "None of your business." But then I think of what I must do next, and I know I can't do it alone. "Do you want to do something exciting?" He studies my face a few seconds before his hands frame my face as he leans in, kissing me. For a minute or two I forget what I was after, but Gabi's face pops up in my head and I shove him away. "Stop it. Think of Gabi."

He looks away, muttering, "I can't when I'm with you."

I hate myself for wanting to believe him. I lean my head on his shoulder. "She's my friend." I whisper.

He turns back to me. "Really?"

I struggle when I remember every time Gabi's given me a rude look or said something mean to me or one of my friends. I shrug uneasily. "I've known her longer." I swallow hard and dig my fingernails into my palms. "I'm not a girl who kisses other girl's boyfriends."

He steps forward, hugs me tight. "You're not?" he whispers in my ear, teasing.

"I don't want to be." I answer into his shoulder before I step away and clap my hands quietly in his face. "Time to focus, Denver. I have a great senior prank plan. Do you want in on it?"

He wrinkles his nose and moves away from my hands. "But you're not a senior."

I drop my hands. "I'm a junior, which is close enough, and this is practice for when I am." I eye him daringly. "You're a senior. Have you pulled any stunts yet?"

He eyes me up and down suggestively. "Where have *you* been?"

I shrug my shoulders, downplaying my anxiety. "I'm still me. Maybe I'm just bored."

He stares a second longer. "Fine. What are we doing?"

I can't help but smile. "I'm going to steal the dummy from the English room closet."

"Why?"

I can't tell him the real reason. "Why not?"

"Fair enough. When are you going to do this?"

I glance down at my watch. It's getting close to midnight. I probably should wait a day to make a better plan, but I'm running out of time. "Now. Let's do it now." He glances past me in the direction of the garage, hesitating, as if trying to make a decision. My stomach clenches. "Why are you here, Denver? How long have you been here?" I watch him carefully, trying to decide if he heard any of Cary and my conversation.

He bites his lip, something he does when he's nervous. "I just got here. Calm down, Ciara. You and Cary must have had *some* conversation."

I try to read him, but he stares blankly back at me. "You're not answering my question."

His eyes fall, and he kicks the dirt. "You didn't answer mine." Our eyes lock once more. The air feels heavy and tense. It's hard to breathe. He breaks the silence. "Come on, Ciara. Are we doing this or not?" He looks around. "How'd you get here?"

I feel silly. "I rode my bicycle."

He goes over, picks it up, and sits down on the seat. "Hop on front. I'll give you a ride."

I look at him, feeling insecure. "I don't think that's a good idea."

He motions with his head. "Come on, small Yengst. This bike's a mongoose. It's sturdy." He taps the handlebars. "I'll fly you to the moon."

I giggle. "You wish." I climb up on the handlebars, feeling like a little girl again. "If you dump me..."

He nips my shoulder. "Don't worry, Ciara, I've got you." He whispers in my ear. My heart flutters in my chest. Boy does he ever.

———

We get to the school, and he takes my hand, leading me around the building. There's something about the way he moves that tells me he's used to sneaking around. "What are you thinking, Nancy Drew?" He mutters in my direction. I smile at the nickname. I love a good mystery.

I clear my throat and answer in kind. "Well, Hardy Boy, I was thinking we go up the fire escape and then walk the ledge around to the government classroom. That window should be open."

He snorts. "Did you prop it or something?"

I giggle. "No, but last year, on the last day of school, Bob and Paul played a joke on Mr. Ash by climbing out the window to hide when he stepped out in the hallway. It was pretty funny." I giggle again at the memory. "Anyway, the dummy idea just came to me today, and I wanted to do it before I lose my nerve."

"Let's get to it then." I follow him around the building, sidling along the brick wall. We round the corner and I rush past him, dropping his hand on the way to the fire escape stairs.

I run up the steps, but then I hear him behind me. I stop, turn back, and whisper-shout, "I need you to be my lookout."

He chuckles low. His long legs eat up the stairs. He reaches for my hand, but I dodge him and go up a few more stairs as he calls after me. "I'm not missing out on all the action."

He's so infuriating. I scold him like a little boy. "This won't work if we both get caught, Denver. I don't have time for arguing. Get back down there." I stretch my arm out like a queen and point toward the empty parking lot.

He smirks up at me and lunges up two stairs to catch up. He gets in my space and breathes softly on my lips. "Then don't argue." He flies past me, and I race to keep up, taking three steps for his one.

We get to the top and he steps out on the ledge first, belly-hugging the side of the building. I follow behind him blindly, keeping my eyes on his hand closest to me as it caresses the wall. He gets to the first window, and tugs on it, but it doesn't budge. I listen for an alarm system to go off, but nothing happens. We continue our ledge walk. He disappears around the corner, and I freeze. I look down. My stomach jumps to my throat. I can't breathe. Time passes, and I feel so stupid. My eyes water. I want to move one foot in front of the other, but I can't.

I'm stuck on the ledge. I've failed my brother and myself. What good is an idea if you can't carry it out? My body trembles as I hug the building, unable to move. It feels like hours have gone by when I see Denver's head around the corner. "Ciara?"

I push the words out. "I can't... I can't move."

He reaches out his hand. "Yes, you can, Ciara. Look at me. Take my hand."

I shake my head. "I can't, Denver. If I let go of the wall, I'll fall. I know it."

"Ciara. Take my hand. Do it for Crash."

I try to let go of the building, but it's like my hand is superglued to the wall.

"Ciara, do it for me." Denver's voice is firm and sure. The confidence in his eyes draws me to him. My foot moves a hair.

I take a deep breath and let it out as I relax my body long enough to reach for his hand. I grasp it, and I'm moving again. I follow him around the corner, only to see the length of the building in front of us. I feel defeated. "At this pace, we won't get to the other side until morning. I'm sorry Denver."

He smiles back at me. "Where there's a will, Ciara, there's a way. You taught me that." I watch as he pulls something from his jacket and pops the window open. He turns back to me, all serious. "Breaking and entering is a family trait, I'm afraid."

I giggle even though I probably shouldn't. "Works for me."

He climbs in through the window, and I follow. We run through the dark school building, holding hands and feeling free. I look over at him and laugh as we run along. I'll never see these classrooms or hallways the same.

We fly up the stairs that lead to the English room, and I trail my fingers along the wall. I run into the chalkboard and follow it to the back of the room until I find the closet doorknob. I throw open the closet door.

Denver stays close, and I'm so glad. This adventure is exciting but being in the classrooms in the dark creeps me out. We stumble into the closet, giggling. "This feels so wrong."

He squeezes my hand. "Yeah, I guess."

I don't know what to make of his words. "What? You make a habit of sneaking into places you don't belong?"

"I don't know. I'm pretty good at it. Besides, didn't Mrs. Umbry say everyone's always welcome here?"

I squeeze his hand hard. "I think she meant during school hours, smarty pants. Not in the middle of the night. Now walk down the middle so we don't knock everything over." We don't get far, and things start falling left and right. I drop his hand, put my hands out to the sides, and try to feel my way. "This closet feels like it's a mile long."

"Yeah. How much time does she spend garage saling?"

I get defensive. Mrs. Umbry is one of my favorite teachers. "So, she loves to reward her students with treasures, so what?"

"Calm down, Ciara. All I'm saying is there's a bunch of crap in here."

I take a deep breath. "We just need to slow down."

"Screw this. I'm turning on my phone light." His voice rumbles behind me. A light flashes just as something pokes me in the nose. I go to scream, but Denver clamps his hand over my mouth as I stare straight into the face of Chucky, the demon doll, sitting on a shelf level with my face. His chubby, offending finger sticks out, touching my cheek. His freaky eyes and creepy grin are forever fixed in my memory. I rip Denver's hand from my face before I grab Chucky by the neck in self-defense, whirl him around, and shove him to the back.

Denver breathes out. "How can you touch that thing?"

"I can't have him staring at me." I answer as I grab his phone hand, pull the light over my shoulder, and point with my opposite hand. "There's the dummy. Go get him."

I try to move sideways, but there's not much room. Denver squeezes past me front-to-front in a full body hug move. He dips his nose in my neck. I feel heat down to my toes. "You smell so good." He goes by me super slow mo.

I give his back a shove. "Shut up, Mr. Smooth-talker, and grab the dummy."

He picks it up. "How am I going to carry this on the ledge?"

I fish around and grab a ball of jute twine. "Follow me." I tiptoe back through the closet, snatch Chucky off the shelf, scalping him. A NASA hat catches my eye. I prop it on his head and put him back on the shelf.

Denver laughs behind me. "You got it in for a doll, Ciara?"

I turn around and slug him lightly in the gut. "It's all part of the master plan, Denver. Keep your eyes on the prize."

We step out of the closet. I take the dummy from him. "He's going piggyback."

"What? He'll fall off."

"I'm going to hog tie him to you." I put the dummy on his back, wrap the arms and legs around Denver, come around Denver's front, and cross the dummy's hands on his chest before tying its wrist tight. I wrap the legs around his waist and do the same with his ankles. I stand back and look him over. "How's that feel?"

Denver jumps up and down. The dummy doesn't fall. "I guess

we're good." He watches as I stuff the wig in my hoodie pocket. "What's with keeping the Chucky doll hair?"

"It's a wig for the dummy."

"Why don't you just glue it on now? I saw super glue in front of the closet."

I grab his phone, use the light to find the glue, and put the twine back on the shelf. "Thanks." I go to do it, but there's a problem. "You're too tall, Denver. Get on your knees so I can see the top of his head."

"Bossy. I like it." He drops to his knees, and I focus on getting the wig on halfway decent. His phone's blowing up with Snaps from Gabi.

I hand it to him. "You going to do something about that?"

He snatches it from me, and I know I'm being nosy, but I can't help but watch out of the corner of my eye as he turns off his location, ghosting Gabi. I smile for a minute, but then I whip my own phone out. I feel stupid as I do the same.

He shuts off his phone light. We leave the classroom hand-in-hand, walking quietly through the hallways. I head back to the math room window. I walk through the middle, while Denver hugs the wall. "It's not smart to walk in the open, you know, in case there's hidden cameras."

I know I should keep my mouth shut, but he just gave me an opening, and I can't forget the weird video in the white box. "What do you know about hidden cameras?"

"I know a little. Come on, get out of the middle of the room, Ciara. You're making me nervous."

I giggle with nervous laughter as I speak low and whispery. "I'd rather walk in the middle, away from the curtains that feel alive as they brush against my skin, and the textbooks sitting on the shelves like they're watching me. Every corner of the room has eyes."

Denver walks a little closer to me. "Stop it, Ciara. How many horror films do you watch?"

I can't help but giggle. "I don't. My imagination is bad enough."

We stop at the window, and he takes my hand. "Are you ready for this?"

I swallow hard. "There's only one way out."

He tilts his head up when he's halfway out the window. "A kiss for good luck?"

I lay my hands on his shoulders and lean in. "If I shove you, you'll reach the ground a whole lot faster." I whisper in his ear.

He backs out sideways and disappears from sight.

Descending happens quickly, as my focus is on the dummy and making sure Denver doesn't fall off the side of the building. We dash down the stairs and high-five when we finally touch ground. "Ha, ha! We did it! Now what?"

I squeeze his bicep. "I need the dummy for a few days."

"What are you gonna do with him?"

I fiddle with my earring, twisting it. "I don't know yet, but I'll find a way to put him to good use." I look back at Denver as we stand in the shadows of the parking lot lights. "I can't believe you scaled the ledge with a dummy on your back."

He laughs. "First time for everything, Nancy Drew." He takes my hand in his. "Let's get you home."

We walk back across the lawn, staying close to the building walls. He hops on the bike, and I take my place on the handlebars, holding on tight. We start down the little hill and his chin rests on my shoulder. "Lean back and let go, Ciara."

I grip the bars tighter. "No, I can't."

"Yeah, you can. Just do it."

I close my eyes. I'm afraid to look as I let go. I raise my arms slowly, loose and free. I lean back against him as he stands on the pedals. "You're crazy, Denver."

His chin rests on my head. I grin from ear to ear. "We're both crazy." He answers into the night.

7

As soon as we're home, I run up my front porch stairs, paranoid I'll be caught. "Ciara. Your dummy."

I wheel around and come back down. "Oh, yeah."

I try to untie the knots, but it's not going well. Denver reaches in his back pocket and pulls out a pocketknife. I step back as he cuts the twine. The dummy falls on the ground. He moves away from it. "Hey, can I borrow your bike? It's kind of late and I've got a long walk."

"Sure. Where you staying? I'll just take the truck and get it tomorrow or something." I feel strange, as I've never asked him where he lives, and he's never said.

He shakes his head. "Nah, that's alright. I'll get it back to you in good time."

"Sure. Okay." I watch him walk away. "Hey, Denver." He turns back and looks up at me, but I can't read his face. "Thanks, again. I couldn't have done it without you."

He laughs and shakes his head. "Yes, you could, Ciara." He folds his knife and puts it away. "There's not much you can't do." He turns around and stands near my front porch light. He's still shaking his head as he gets on my bike to ride away.

I walk inside and drag the dummy behind me, muttering to myself. "I can't stay away from Denver. That's one thing I can't do."

I take the dummy to my room, toss him in a chair, and fall into bed.

I wake to a knocking on my door. I glance over at the clock. It's 6:30 a.m. Char sticks her head in. "Wake up, Ciara. Family meeting. Now."

I rub the sleep from my eyes. I look down and see I'm still wearing

45

my clothes from the night before. Char's eyes fly to the dummy. "Where'd that come from? How long has it been here?"

Thank goodness Char respects my privacy. I mumble at her, feeling half asleep. "It's for a school play for English. It's a character study."

She shakes her head and rolls her eyes. "Downstairs, now."

I stumble down the stairs half asleep and plop down at the kitchen table. "Where's Crash?"

She mutters, "I'm going to get him."

Six and a half minutes later, but who's counting, Char walks back in the kitchen with a dripping-wet Crash stomping in behind her. "You didn't have to throw water on me!"

She throws up her hands. "I've got a job to get to on time, but this was important!" Crash drops in a chair and rests his head on his arms. Char slams a cup of water down by him along with two aspirins before smacking the back of his head. "For your hangover, sweetie."

Crash cradles his head. "Char, keep it down."

Char turns her glare on me. "Why's Crash's truck not in the driveway?"

I stare at her across the table. "Why are you looking at me?"

Crash raises his head and turns sideways to lay his cheek on his arm. "I told you. I lent it to a friend." He answers tiredly.

"And would this be the *same* friend who took it down a creek bed and left a dead body behind!" Char's voice is louder than I've ever heard.

Crash looks up. "No."

Char crosses her arms. Her eyes dart between Crash and me. "The two of you know something. You know how I know you know something?" She pauses, staring us down. "Neither of you seem a bit surprised by this information!"

Crash turns his bowed head to look at her sideways. "And how do you know any of this is even true?"

She purses her lips. "Let's just say I heard it from a reliable source."

Crash smacks the table hard. "Cary! I told him..."

I cut him off with a glare and a shake of my head. Char pounces on him. "You told him what, Crash? Why are you talking to Cary?"

I clear my throat. "We found the truck in the creek bed, Char. Um, Tom borrowed it, but he didn't bring it back, so we got worried."

She smacks her hands on her arms. "So I suppose you two already know that Tom got shot yesterday and he's now in the county jail for shooting the man in your truck."

Crash's eyes get huge. "Tom's in jail? That was quick!"

Char narrows her eyes at Crash. "It sounds like you already knew Tom shot him."

I take a breath and choose my words carefully. "We knew Tom got shot, but I thought he was still in the hospital."

She glances at the kitchen wall clock. "I've got to get to work. You two stay home today. No going anywhere."

My phone's blowing up. I turn it over. "Char, I've got a fundraiser at the high school this morning."

She stares me down. "You're not going."

Good. I don't want to, but I can't give in this easily. "I better go. It'll look suspicious if I don't."

She nods her head. "Fine, but you leave your 365 tracker on the whole time."

Crash clears his throat. "I'm supposed to work today."

Char gives him a dirty look. "Then don't be late."

I look between the two of them. "If he takes my car to work, how will I get to the school?"

She turns back to me. "I guess you'll have to ride your bike."

"But my bike is..." I stop, remembering everything from the night before. "Fine."

I race back upstairs to get ready; shower and braid my hair. I grab a pop tart on the way out the door.

Char calls after me. "We're so not done talking about this!"

8

I walk/jog to the school. I'm thankful for the distraction until I see Gabi's face as I walk into the concession stand. Great. She blocks the doorway with her hand on her hip. "Just what were you doing at the school this morning at 1:30 a.m. with *my boyfriend*?"

I breeze past her. "I have no idea what you're talking about, Gabi. I was home in bed."

"You've got bags under your eyes, and you look tired. Your Snapchat location was the same as Denver's."

"Then why don't you just ask Denver." I can't believe how flippant I'm being, but right now my world seems a whole lot bigger than being afraid of Gabi.

She glances sideways and looks as if she might cry. "I'm asking you."

I guess my patience is gone because my words just keep flying. "I've got no answers for you, Gabi. The burritos are callin' my name."

I glance over at Ari, hoping for some support. "They're enchiladas, Ciara. Get over here and start filling."

I wash my hands and throw on a pair of gloves, happy to escape Gabi's glare. "Hey, Ari."

Ari hip bumps me. "What's up, Ciara. Have you been ghosting us?"

I don't know what to say. "I'm not trying to. I've just been kind of busy I guess."

Ari shoulder bumps me. She's feeling exceptionally bumpy today.

"That's cool. Hey, did you finish your math homework? There were a few I had questions on. I thought we could compare."

"Yeah, definitely."

Aaron slides up behind us. "Hey, did I hear math comparisons? Can I get in on this?"

Ari sneers at him. "Not unless you did your homework first."

He throws up his hands and steps away. "Chillax, Ari. Sheesh."

She watches him walk away. "*That's* what I thought." She mutters at Aaron's back. She turns back to me with wide eyes. "So, did you hear the rumor?"

My stomach clenches. "I don't know, what rumor?"

She leans in, whispering quietly, "About your brother's truck found with a body in it."

I look back at her and try to catch my breath and play it cool; but I'm in disbelief. I can't believe she just put that out there. "Ari, not now, okay?"

She frowns at me. "Fine. I was just trying to give you a heads up."

I glance back at her. I hate myself for questioning her actions, but I've got to trust someone, so I answer quietly. "Thanks."

She studies me for a few seconds, but I can't say anymore. "So, I think I'll go dress shopping soon. What about you?"

I shrug. "I don't know. I hadn't thought too much about it yet." We finish filling the enchiladas. I remember I left something on Friday. "I'm going to the bathroom. I'll be right back."

I run up the stairs to my locker, open it to grab my notebook, and that's when I see another box sitting there. I look up and down the halls. I see no one. I think back to last night. Denver was with me the whole time unless he broke in before. It has to be him, right? I grab the box with shaking hands and shove it in a plastic bag lying on the bottom of my locker. I walk down the stairs and leave through a side door. I hate to bail, but I have to go home. I can't wait another minute to find out what's on this video.

I rush home, run up the stairs, and start up my laptop.

The old lady's back. She lies in her bed, staring out the window. She seems more relaxed as her fingers dangle over the side of her bed.

The man approaches. He knocks her food tray away. She turns toward him with a strange calm. "He shot the Bulldog. He will pay." The man growls.

She smiles up at him. "I told you to give him time. The Bulldog shouldn't have let his guard down."

The man's fists clench at his sides. "He had enough time to pay me. He'd been warned. His time was up."

"So, he got away." She answers, as if she didn't know. Do I imagine a look of relief on her face?

"Well, kind of, yes. But I believe he's wounded." The man sounds frustrated.

"Wounded but alive. He's a survivor. I'm a survivor, too." There's emotion in her voice, but it's hard to read. "What's your next step?"

"I don't know. He took one of mine, I've got to take one of his." His words chill me to the bone. Is someone coming after Tom?

"What if he works alone?"

"Everyone has their weaknesses. I'll find his."

The woman twitches in her bed. One hand lays over the side, but her other is hidden. "Did the Bulldog force his hand?" Her words are measured.

"Jimmy was just doing his job!"

"He didn't do it well enough. Now he's unemployed." There's a trace of humor in her voice.

"He's dead."

She raises her dangling hand, palm up. "Those are the hazards of a hired hand. Chasing the crown can be a bloody business." The woman suffers a coughing spell. She covers her mouth with linen and fights to keep her focus on the man. "Your time will come. Keep your eyes on the prize."

The man approaches the lady, leans over, and casts a shadow. "I intend to." He reaches out and squeezes her hand hard enough to make her wince. "My time is near."

I shut it off. I'm not sure what to make of it, but I'm unable to watch any more. It's hard to believe this is a video of real people, and who is filming this horror show? Why are they sending these things to me? I throw the card back in the box and shove it in my bag. I cram it in the back of my closet. I stand up. I have to get out of here. If I stay in my room, my thoughts will make me crazy. I pick up my phone and go back to the school.

The rest of the morning goes okay. I manage to avoid Gabi as we make more enchiladas and clean the kitchen in between.

I'm headed down the hallway to go home a second time when someone grabs my hand and pulls me behind me a door. "Ciara."

I follow Denver's voice. "What are you doing?"

"I have to talk to you."

"Here?" Now that the door's shut, there's absolutely no light.

"Yes. Gabi will think I'm here at the fundraiser." His breath feels hot on my cheek, but there's no way to get away from him.

My heart races and my palms feel itchy. I grab a hold of my tee shirt for something to hold onto. "What do you need, because we can't be caught in the closet."

"I didn't know it was a closet." Every time he speaks, his breath touches me again.

"What is going on?" His smell is so delicious.

"I don't know. I heard Tom's in jail."

"Yeah, I heard that too." Why is his hand on my hip, and why don't I brush it away?

"What happened?" What was the question; he smells so good I can't think straight. This is so hard trying to figure out who knows what. "Ciara?"

I take a breath. "I'm not sure. Someone stole my brother's truck yesterday, and it ended up in the creek bed with a dead body in it." My voice cracks. I'm on the edge of falling apart.

Denver squeezes my arm and draws me closer, if that's possible. "What? You knew all of this last night and you didn't tell me?" His breath is near my ear and on my neck. Could I have possibly heard hurt in his tone? Surely not.

"Denver, I need some space." He doesn't move. "I didn't tell you, because there was a body."

He holds me tight, and I want to stay here forever. "Are you okay, Ciara?"

My lip trembles, and it's hard to stay mad at him when he's like this, but if I let go of my shirt, my hands will be on Denver, and I don't know if I'll be able to let go. "Don't worry about me, I'll be fine." No, I'm not fine. Someone's sending me bizarre videos of a sadist in a hospital bed, and I think it's Denver. I shove away from him. "I've got to go."

I open the door and spy Ari down the hallway. I reach around him, grab a roll of toilet paper, and hold it up like an idiot. "Found it." I give Denver a hard shove backwards before I shut the door on him and run down the hallway to the exit.

9

I run up the steps to Crash's apartment and bust in. "Crash!"

He looks up from his couch nest of beer and potato chips. "What?"

I pinch his neck hard. "Sober up. We're going to Cary's in an hour. We've got be ready when the guy calls back."

Crash rubs the pink spot on his neck. "Damn, Ciara. Don't pinch me so hard. I've got something you might want to hear."

I really don't think so. "Oh?"

"Yeah. I went to see Walkman at the jail. I recorded our conversation on purpose this time."

"And you want me to hear it?"

He looks back at me. "You're the mad scientist."

I plop down on the end of his sofa. "You've got that right."

He lays his phone down between us and pushes play. I hear Tom's voice. He almost sounds excited. "You should have seen it, Crash. I mean, I walked right in here like I owned the place. I looked that deputy in the eye, and said, 'Aren't you going to read me my rights?' I mean, that's what they do on the cop shows. So the guy mirandizes me, and I tell him I don't want an attorney. I go, I've got something to say. My name is Tom Edwards, otherwise known as Walkman. I'm twenty-two years old. I live on the side of a highway in an apartment.

Today, I took Jimmy's gun from him and shot him in the chest. He died. I'm here to accept my punishment. Doris Dunham is my landlord. She will need to know where I am and that I cannot pay her rent. My mom lives in a Rehab Center, and they will need to know I can't pay them either. But please don't tell them until next month because I already paid them for this month. And that's all I have to say." There's a pause. "After that, the deputy walked my happy butt back to a holding cell, and I laid down on the bench and went to sleep. Since then, I've been eating three meals a day, watching a little tellie, and enjoying my status of killing a hitman."

Crash stops the video. "So that's it. He went right in and confessed."

I shake my head. "He's probably more afraid of who's on the outside than who's on the inside."

Crash looks over at me. "You really think so?"

I nod my head. "Crash, he shot a hitman! That can't be good. And there's the whole money situation."

Someone knocks on the door, and I fly off the couch. Crash pulls out a gun from beneath the couch cushion. What is going on? I run for the bathroom, open the window, and stick my head out. There's no ledge and I'm two stories up. Dang it.

Crash's voice calls out loud and clear. "Hey, Cary."

I flush the toilet and run the water before joining them in the living room.

Cary looks over at my brother. "Man, I haven't been by here in at least a year."

Crash looks over at Cary warily. "What's going on? Why are you here?"

Cary eyes him right back. "I don't know. Why don't you tell me? Did you know Walkman's locked up at the county jail? He's so happy, he was practically singing."

Crash glares back at him. "How do you know what's going on at the jail?"

Cary shifts uncomfortably. "Let's just say I know someone on the inside. What's it matter to you? I mean, with the trouble it looks like you might be in, I think you'd be glad to know what's going on."

Crash stares at the floor. "You know, Cary, it wasn't that long ago, and you could have been in Walkman's shoes. I mean, for all I know, you're his competition."

"Fair enough, Crash. I hear what you're saying, and I'm not disagreeing. But you're going to have to trust me when I say I'm not in that line of work anymore. I saw the light." Cary's voice is flat and even.

Crash snorts. "Yeah, you saw the light, Cary; somewhere between house arrest and community service."

Cary jumps up. His face turns red. "Make all the smartass comments you want, Crash. But you're in a heap of trouble right now, and I sure as hell didn't help you get there! Now you can keep this up, keep being your stupid, stubborn self, or you could pull your head out of your ass and take the hand I'm trying to extend to you."

My brother doesn't back off. "What's in it for you, Cary? Why would you want to help me, since you're all about walking the straight-and-narrow now?"

"I haven't forgotten we were friends back in the day," Cary says with a sigh. "I know what it's like to make a mistake or two. I just don't want to see you continue down that road until you're in so deep it's too late. So, I'm asking you again. Why was Walkman practically begging to be locked up?"

I step into the conversation. "Maybe he's just happy to have a free meal and a warm bed."

Cary looks at me with a doubtful expression. "I'm going to pretend I heard no sarcasm in your voice. It seemed like Walkman was running from someone or something. It felt like he was wanting protection."

Crash is on his feet. "You saw the dead body! And I already *told* you Walkman and that dude left my yard in my truck! Maybe Walkman was being held against his will! Maybe he needed protection but didn't know how to get it, or it was too late for him. Speaking of protection; why are you so buddy-buddy with the deputy? There used to be a time when you couldn't stand the cops."

Cary snorts. "We're back on that again? There was also a time when we were all young and stupid. I've outgrown that phase. Have you?"

Crash crosses his arms on his chest. "What's that supposed to mean?"

"It means have you gotten yourself into some kind of trouble, the kind you can't get out of?"

"No. Why would you think that?"

"I don't know. Maybe 'cause there was a dead guy in your truck, and you didn't seem too surprised."

"I could ask the same of you, you know. I mean, how is it you got there so fast, and you didn't seem at all surprised to find the dead man either?"

Cary taps his fingers on his elbows. "I already told you. I heard it on the scanner."

Crash takes a deep breath and stares back at Cary. "Well. If that's your story, mine is just what I told the deputy today. Walkman needed my truck. He's never asked before, so I figured it was legit. He borrowed it. I saw him take off with that guy, Jimmy. They left and didn't come back. So, I went looking for it. End of story."

Cary keeps his eyes on my brother. "If you say so. But if you don't ask for help, no one can help you. And if you're hiding something, Crash, the truth will come out."

Crash sits in silence a long time sipping his beer. "Well, I've said all I need to say."

Cary gets up. "You always were too stubborn for your own good." He walks toward the door, but then he stops to look back at us. "And Crash? I never said his name was Jimmy."

Oh, crap. I can't believe Crash slipped up like that, and Cary caught it, and neither can Crash, as he looks back at Cary. "You really have been hanging around the station too long."

I clap my hands at the two of them. "Alright now. That's enough. We've got to get this plan going."

Crash looks back at me, all worried. "He wants to meet tonight in the barn."

"What? Are you serious? Why didn't you tell me? What time? We've got to get things ready!"

Cary walks back toward me. "Do you have what you need, Ciara?"

Crash looks at me and then Cary. "You're involving him?"

I look back at my brother. I'm completely ticked off that he got me in this mess and that he expects me to fix it. "Crash. Number one, don't ask me to do something and then tell me how to do it. Two; I told you we can't do this alone. I trust Cary. I need both of you to make this work."

Cary nods in agreement before turning on Crash. "And three, don't wait 'till the last minute and expect us to work miracles, idiot."

Crash makes a face at me. "You sound just like Char."

I sneer back at him. "Good. At least she knows how to get the job done."

Cary looks at me and then Crash. "Alright, you two, it's go time. Let's get to work on the plan. Crash, when this is all done, you're getting out of town. I know a place."

Crash sits back down. "How do you know a place, and what about my job?"

I want to choke my brother myself as I answer. "Crash, if you're not here, you can't work." I turn to Cary. "You were talking about a hiding place?"

Cary goes to the window and looks out. "Crash, as I said, I've been where you are, and someone helped me once. You're going to have to lay low for a while. So if you have any books or cards, I suggest you take them."

Crash frowns. "No T.V.?"

Cary looks back at Crash. "No noise." There's an awkward silence. "And, Crash, your life is worth more than your job."

Crash has the sense to look down at the floor a few seconds, but then he jumps up, startling both of us. He takes one last swig of his beer before he chucks it in the trash can across the room. "Let's go get ready for my hangin'."

———

Against my better judgment, I Snap Ari. I'm having doubts, and if this all goes south, I'm going to need major help. "Be at the old barn in the pasture tonight at 10 by the edge of the woods. I need a witness. I'm depending on you to keep your mouth shut."

I breathe easy when I get a thumbs up.

Cary, Crash, and I practice most of the afternoon. I can't believe I'm perfecting how a dummy swings from the rafters to make it as realistic as possible. About the third time, Crash speaks up. "We're going to have to put my shoes and hat on him, in case the guy looks too closely. Ciara, are you sure you can face him?"

I look up at Crash, who sits high in the rafters above the hanging dummy. I swallow hard and wish for nerves of steel. "I can do this."

I unpack a supper. We sit around like three blind mice, nibbling our cheese and apples. I glance over at Cary. "Thanks for doing this, Cary. I really appreciate it."

Cary coughs. "I'm not doing this for you. I'm doing it for Char."

Crash kicks his knee lightly and laughs. "When are you going to tell her what we did?"

Cary laughs. "Never. I think I'll just tell her I got you out of a jam."

I smile. "It sounds like you know her pretty well."

Cary drops his apple. "There was a time when I did."

"She's still the Char you knew. She just has more stress and responsibility now." I can't believe I'm confiding in Cary about Char. She'd kill me if she knew. We both eye Crash accidentally.

Crash throws down his apple. "Don't you two gang up on me! I never wanted this to happen." He takes a drink of pop, sets it down, and shakes his head. "Tom's not a bad guy. He just got mixed up."

Cary sets down his plate. "He murdered someone, Crash. After this week, I have no idea who Tom really is."

Crash isn't done. "It was self-defense!" He taps his knee nervously. "He just went too far down the wrong path."

I stare off into space., "He's not the only one who's lost." I get up. "Come on, let's practice again. We can't afford to screw this up."

We go through it a few more times, and then we wait. Ten o'clock comes and goes, and I think he's on to us, but then he shows up at 10:30. Just when I think I'll finally see his face, I'm wrong. He wears a creepy President's mask, but I feel his eyes boring into me.

"Who are you?" I ask with a trembling voice.

"I'm The Neighbor." His answer leaves no more room for questions. "I'm here for the money or the kid who owes me."

I swallow hard. Crash is the kid. "I'm… I'm the kid's sister. He told me to meet him here, but..."

The man creeps closer. My heart pounds in my chest. The dummy swings through the air. I scream louder than I ever have in my life and hold out my hands. "Crash! Nooo." I fall to the ground, bawling as I cover my face with my hands.

There's a presence. All I see are his shoes as he steps into a shaft of light that lights the ground in front of me on the dirt floor. "It's done, then. Blood for money." His words are a little shaky. He turns to go. His footsteps quiet as he exits.

I nod my head at the floor. I can't look up. I'm chilled. to the bone. I stay where I am and cry into the dirt until I hear a car drive away.

I pop up my head and wait for Cary. Crash cuts down the dummy, who falls to the floor. He crosses the rafters and comes down to stand beside me. Cary steps out of the shadows, looking a little shaken. "You're a little too convincing, Ciara."

I stare at the dummy lying lifeless on the floor. "Thanks." I walk over, remove its shoes and hat and hand them to my brother. "Put these back on."

He chuckles. "No repeat performances?"

I give him a hard shove. "You're not funny, Crandall."

Cary laughs out loud. "Crandall?"

Crash punches him hard in the shoulder. "Say it again."

Cary rubs his shoulder and steps back. "Cran-berry juice."

Crash drops his fist. "You're so funny."

Cary picks up the dummy. "Alright, guys. Let's walk back to the truck. Tonight's not over. I've got some serious driving to do."

10

W e get back to the house. Crash runs up to get his stuff from his apartment. I take the dummy in and walk through the living room in the dark. I about fall over when the chair in the corner makes noise. A voice comes out of the darkness. "Hey, Ciara."

"Oh, hey, Char. You scared me."

She walks toward me, looking all weird. "Did I? I get the impression not much does."

I want so badly to unload on her. "What do you mean?"

She flips on a lamp. I feel foolish for standing around in the dark. "What are you doing with a dummy at this time of the night?"

"I don't know. Just pulling a senior prank."

"You're not a senior yet."

I dance back and forth. "I will be soon enough."

She glares at me. "Look, I'm going with Cary and Crash. Cary told me Crash got in a jam, and he's trying to help him out by taking him somewhere safe. I'd like to wring Crash's neck for whatever mess he's gotten into, but that won't do any good. I'm at the end of my rope with him." I wince at her choice of words.

I want so much to tell Char it's not all his fault, but then I'd have to tell her what I did. "Char, please don't be too hard on Crash. He has the best of intentions, and I have a feeling this wasn't all his fault. It could be a fluke, like being at the wrong place at the wrong time."

She watches me carefully, and I know that look. She's about to ask me twenty questions, but I'm saved by her phone blowing up. "That's

Cary. I gotta go. He says he's leaving now. I'm only riding with him so I'll know where Crash is."

I go to tease her, but I don't. I'm too relieved to not be the only one worrying about my brother. "Thanks, Char."

She squeezes my shoulder. "We will have a talk about tonight."

I nod my head up and down like a bobble head. "Okay."

I run upstairs and toss the dummy in the spare room. I can't stand to look at it any longer. I run downstairs to flip the lock before taking a quick shower. I need to rinse off everything that just happened. I feel somewhat refreshed. I throw on my comfy sweats and hoodie and curl up on the couch downstairs.

There's a knock at the door. I flip off the TV and run to the bathroom to hide. Given everything I've just been through, I can't take any more unexpected visitors. I wish I had Crash's gun. I shake my head. I can't believe I want a gun! My phone buzzes in my hand. "Nancy Drew. It's Hardy Boy. Let me in."

I run back to the front door, turn on the porch light, and peer through the window. I smile down at Denver's signature baby blue Vans standing on my Welcome Mat. I flip the locks and open the door. He steps in and runs his hands through his hair.

I look up at him, and that's all it takes for me to fall apart as he reaches for me. His hands cradle my chin, and his lips meet mine. I step into him as I feel the first real teardrop of the night roll down my cheek. He steps away, breathing hard. "I'm sorry. I just had to know you were okay." His voice is all husky, and I'm so confused.

"What do you mean?"

"I was there, Ciara. I was at the barn tonight."

My head reels. "Whhat? Why?"

"I was with Gabi. You contacted Ari?"

"Yeah. I didn't know what to do, and I was worried about things getting really bad. It was selfish of me, I know. But I didn't know what else to do. I thought Ari would come alone."

His hands hit against his pockets. "Well apparently she didn't have the nerve to go alone, so she invited Gabi, who then invited me and Raul."

"What?"

He sighs and sits down at the bar. "Yeah. So Gabi, Ari, Raul, and me all saw the hanging."

I sit down. "Oh."

He looks across the bar at me. "It was the dummy, right? That's why you wanted the dummy from the closet."

I fiddle with the salt-shaker lid. "Yeah."

He clears his throat. "Who's the guy in the mask?"

"I don't know."

"What's your brother gotten himself into, Ciara?"

"I don't know."

He takes my hands in his. "What *do* you know?" I hesitate to answer as I try to choose the right words. He wraps his hands around mine and holds them tight. "Ciara, don't do this to me. I can see you're sorting out what to tell me. Don't do it. Just tell me what you know."

I look back at him, frustrated. I take my hands back and stand up. "I know that you keep kissing me even though you're with Gabi. That's what I know."

He slaps the table with his hand. "I'm sorry, okay? I just... I just need to be with her right now. It's for your own safety."

I glare at him. "What does that mean?"

"I can't tell you."

I make a face. "Now who's withholding information."

He walks around the bar to stand in front of me. "That's not fair, Ciara. I'm trying to keep you safe."

I throw up my hands. "All I can tell you is my brother is safe, but as far as you know, he's... he's dead. And the rumors of a dead body found in his truck are true, but he didn't do it. Crash is no murderer." I study Denver. I wish I knew which side he is on.

Denver comes closer. He pulls me to him. "I believe you. It's going to be okay, Ciara. You have to trust me."

I lean on his chest. I hate my weakness when it comes to Denver. "When? When is it going to be okay?"

"You have to be patient."

I sigh. "I don't have *time* to be patient."

He steps away from me to open my fridge. He grabs a bottle of water and hands me one. He snoops through our pantry for snacks and grabs a bag of chips. "Sit with me and breathe a minute. Let's watch some Netflix."

I know I shouldn't, as I'm already in hot water with Gabi over Denver, but I shove that thought away as I curl up next to him on the couch, feeling all cozy. It's nice to forget everything for a while. Denver's the only person I know who I can be myself with. He accepts me for who I am.

———

The next thing I know, it's morning. I wake up sprawled on top of Denver, and I can't help but feel that we fit just right. I know I shouldn't, but I lay my cheek back on his chest, close my eyes, and burrow back in. Minutes later, the front door flies open. A red-faced Char comes barreling in. She drops her keys on a chair, and barely glances our way as she tears through the house. "Ciara, make me some coffee please. I've got to shower before work."

I peel myself off Denver and wonder how he can sleep through all her noise. I'm halfway off the couch when I see his one eye peek open. He gives me a little smirk before he turns over to bury his face under a couch pillow. I race to the kitchen to start the coffee before I run to grab an Afghan from the hall closet, which I take and toss over the side of the couch. I hurry back to the kitchen to start some scrambled eggs and toast for Char, who does a kitchen run-by, tossing her eggs in a paper bowl and sloshing her coffee in a to-go cup.

She pauses by the couch and looks back at me. Her eyebrows are raised in question. I manage to look her in the eye, shake my head back and forth, and blush a little as she leans down to whisper a threat in Denver's ear. She turns back to me. "Ciara, be careful. I'll see you tonight."

It feels strange to know Denver spent the night with me. All I want to do is crawl back on the couch with him and forget the world and all the trouble I'm in, but I can't do that. I feel a pair of eyes on me. I look over to see him peeking over the couch and smiling a sleepy smile. My heart melts all over again. "Hey."

I choke. "Hey. You, um, want some breakfast?"

"Sure. I'm just gonna."

"Oh, sure. Bathroom's down that hallway. You'll see it."

I go to the fridge and grab some sausage links and a few more eggs. I find the Mexican cheese to crumble on top of the eggs, add a little milk and a few tablespoons of salsa. I toss the sausage in a separate pan. I turn to find Denver sitting at the bar. "Smells delicious."

I blush again. "Thanks." I look around. "Do you want some coffee?"

He wrinkles his nose. "I'm not really much of a coffee drinker. I like tea with milk."

I pour myself some coffee and add creamer to it. I grab a coffee cup and hand it to him. "The hot water's in the water stand in the corner, and the tea's up in that cupboard." I look back at him. "What are you thinking?"

He coughs. "I was going to ask what you thought about me staying in your brother's place while he's gone."

My heart turns over with the thought of Denver living that close. "Because?"

"Well, I think it'd be better if I found somewhere else to stay for a bit, given all that's going on."

I look at him. "Are you in some sort of trouble?"

He looks away from me. "Not any more trouble than you are."

I take a sip and stand by the sink. "That's not too reassuring."

He takes a step toward me, never breaking his gaze. "Ciara."

"Denver."

"Do you trust me?"

I swallow hard. "I trust you enough, I think."

"What does that mean?"

"It means you can stay above the garage."

"Don't you have to ask Char?"

I choke on my coffee and set the cup down. "I thought you would ask her."

He laughs. "I don't know about that."

I look at him again. "What did she say to you this morning?"

He looks down at the counter. "She told me to keep it in my pants."

My eyes try to focus on anything but his mouth. "Oh."

"Yeah. So…"

"Alright. I'll ask her. You want some breakfast?"

He steps over to the stove and I hand him a paper plate, but he just stands there. "What do I do with the pan lids?"

I chuckle. "That's what my dad used to say." I reach past him, brushing his arm as I grab the lids, laying them sideways in the drainer. "There." I grab a rubber spatula and hand it to him. "For the eggs. Just fork your sausages but don't scrape the fork on the pan."

I step back. I need some air. This all feels so intimate. I sit down at the table and watch him. I can't help but giggle.

He looks at me. "What's so funny?"

I laugh out loud. "I think I'll let *you* tell Gabi why you're staying here."

He sits down with his food. "Oh, crap, Gabi. She's going to be so pissed."

I take a bite of my eggs. "That's the understatement of the year."

We eat in silence for a few minutes before he meets my eyes again across the table. "What's the next step?"

I gaze back at him. "What's that?"

"In the plan. What's the next step?"

"I don't know."

11

I'm outside in the car face-timing Char, which I know isn't the best idea, as she hates calls at work, but she won't be home for another 6 ½ hours, and this can't wait.

She answers, smiling. "What's up Ciara?"

I sit on my fingers to keep from biting my nails; a nervous habit I have only when I'm really stressed, and one she hates. "I, um, have a favor to ask."

"What is it?" Her voice changes, already losing some of its sweetness.

"Well, Denver needs a place to stay for a little while, just until things settle down, and since Crash is gone…"

Her eyes go wide. "You want Denver to stay in Crash's apartment?"

I look sideways. "Please, Char. He's got nowhere to go."

"Ciara Onyx Yengst."

I roll my eyes. "Charlotte Russe Yengst."

She points a finger at the phone. "Don't you take that tone with me. You know I hate these talks as it is, but someone has to."

I wipe a tear away at the rare acknowledgment of the obvious absence of our mother. My brain fogs over for a second or two and I take a deep, reorienting breath. "What?"

Her voice softens. "Ciara, I'm not saying no. I'm saying I have to trust you to make the right decision, here. I know how you feel about him."

I'm so tired of everyone thinking they know everything as I spit out my words, striking back. "How is this any different from you and Cary?"

She sits patiently waiting for me to really look at her. "Ciara, I'm going to say something and I'm going to count on you to not throw it in my face in the future, okay?" Where is this calmness coming from, and why won't she just yell at me? That'd be a lot easier to take than this strange side of Char I haven't seen. What is she talking about? I'm mad that I've forgotten the question, so I just nod my head.

"You know Cary made terrible decisions in the past, but what you don't know is I was headed right down that path with him. It took us losing our parents for me to get my head on straight."

I shake my head. "I don't understand."

This is perfect, dependable, Char we're talking about, which she must have read on my face, as she sighs. "I was steps away from getting in the car that night with Cary, the night he got in serious trouble. The only thing that stopped me from going with him was the call on my phone from the police department after their wreck." I can barely look at her, because if I do, I'm afraid we'll both break down, so I stare out the window. "Ciara, look at me."

I turn back to the phone and stare into her grey eyes, the same color as mine, but that's where the resemblance ends. Char has mom's tiny nose, perfect lips, and dad's shockingly blond hair that curves around her heart-shaped face perfectly. She looks like a Swedish Christmas card or something. I, on the other hand, feel more like a curvaceous Pippi long-stocking. My slightly wavy hair's never in place. I have too many freckles, a pointy nose above a big mouth with a pronounced chin, and somehow managed to inherit boobs that would be enough for three women.

"Ciara."

I snap out of it. "What?"

"All I'm saying is think about who or what you anchor to. The right guy will put the wind in your sails, but the wrong one can get you real stuck, real fast, and before you know it, you're going down with him."

I know I shouldn't, but I giggle. "I didn't know you were such a sailor, Char."

"Damn it, Ciara! I'm trying to look out for you, and I'm not sure Denver is. He may just be looking out for himself."

I look down at the steering wheel. "We're just friends, Char. He has a girlfriend. I'm just trying to help him."

She snorts. "Ciara, friends don't spoon together on the couch like a couple of human blankets." My face heats up, and I can't speak, but that's okay because she's not done. "I'm just saying guard your heart. Guys like Denver can sneak up on a girl, and before you know it, you're shattered. Trust me, I know."

I look at her, feeling selfish that I never saw her pain. "I'm sorry you got hurt, Char."

She takes a deep breath. "Just because we Yengsts have tough exteriors doesn't mean our hearts aren't soft." She glances sideways, blinking. "Now, enough of this... I gotta get back to work." She turns back to the screen, eyes twinkling. "Remember what I said. Don't go so far down the path you can't find your way back. There's a lot of mountains in Denver, you wouldn't want to get lost." She giggles.

I stick out my tongue at her. "Ha ha, very funny."

She laughs out loud. "Love you."

I take a deep breath. "So can he stay?"

She rolls her eyes. "Yes, he can stay. In Crash's apartment. And I'm trusting you to behave."

A squeal escapes me as I jump out of the car. I hear Char's muttering. "Oh no, what have I done."

———

Like everything else that has been on a continual downhill spiral that's out of my control, two hours after Denver moves into Crash's apartment, I lose half my school friends on Snapchat, or at least it feels that way, well everyone but Ari and Esmee. I barely have time to think about it before receiving a message from Ari.

"Gabi's telling everyone Denver cheated on her with you and he's living at your place. Is this true?"

I don't know how to answer, because technically it's all true, but then I remember Ari and Gabi both saw the fake hanging. How could Ari be asking me this question in a time like this? I put the phone away. I've got bigger worries than that. I need to talk to someone, but I can't talk to my friends, not about this. I need Crash, but I don't even know where he is, and Cary said no contact until he returns.

I run back to Crash's apartment, feeling weird as I knock on the door. Seconds later, it's opened by a shirtless Denver, who's got a tattoo on his ribcage that I've never seen before. My eyes skim over the sword going up his side with a date inscribed on the blade as he turns away, tugging on a shirt. "Hey."

I stare at him. "Hi. I guess Gabi figured out where you are."

He frowns. "I told her."

"Why?"

"She was blowing up my phone about the barn and wanting to know why I was here all night."

I tap my fingertips on the doorframe, feeling nervous. "What did you tell her?"

He bites his lip. "As little as possible."

"Which is?"

He sighs. "I told her Crash is my friend, and I need to be close to your family right now."

I nod my head. "I guess that's okay."

He drops his head. "Yeah, but I may have made a bigger mistake on purpose."

I walk by him and sit down on Crash's futon. "What does that mean?"

"I kind of snapped a picture of us on the couch this morning while you were sleeping, and I may have sent it to her, so she kind of thinks I'm living in your house and not above the apartment."

My head's going to explode. "What?"

He takes a deep breath. "Just hear me out. If Gabi thinks we're together, she'll probably be more focused on that fact than what she saw in the barn."

I sigh. "What about Ari and Raul?"

He looks at the wall. "I'm leaving them to you. You'll have to decide how much you trust them and how much you can tell them."

I can't take much more of this. "Denver, just how big do you think my shoulders are?"

"What?" He stares at my shoulders as if something's growing there.

"You're letting everyone believe that I'm a cheater. I've already lost friends on Snapchat over this."

He looks impassive. "Then they're not really your friends."

I jump up. I feel all itchy and irritated. It's like he's not hearing me. "Denver, that's not really the point. There's a whole double standard when it comes to girls who cheat and guys who cheat. You *know* this. Half the school probably thinks I'm a slut right now."

He walks over to me, and I wish he wouldn't. He stands in front of me. His thumb brushes my lip, and I want to nibble it. My sister's words of warning are somewhere in my mind, but right now they sound like a distant echo. "Ciara, when you find the right person, you'd lose everything for them." His words fall on my ears about the time he steps up closer to me.

I hear and feel nothing but the wall of heat that crashes down on me as Denver's lips touch mine. I want him so badly, I'm shaking. His phone goes off, and I step away. I go to the sink for a glass of water while I try to gather myself.

I turn to face him. "What are we going to do?"

He smiles, and I want to kiss him and slap him at the same time. "About what?"

"About the problem. The money. I don't believe the guy's just going to leave me alone, especially now that he's seen my face."

"Why does Crash owe him money?"

I study his face, trying to decide if he's lying to me, but I've got no one else. "Crash had something. I found it. I thought Crash was doing something he shouldn't and so I got rid of it."

He sits down. "Got rid of it how?"

I look sideways, feeling foolish all over again. "I threw it in the river."

"So it washed away?"

"I don't know. I weighted it down with rocks and tried to throw it somewhere deep."

He jumps up. "So it might still be there?"

"I guess."

"Well, we just gotta find it! If we find it, we can give it back to the guy from the barn."

"Denver, it's not that simple. I threw it in the water." Why isn't he hearing me?

"I know, but what other choice do we have?"

"I don't know." He kind of has a point.

"I've got a buddy who fishes. He's got some nets. We can drag the river."

I look at him. "Won't people wonder why we're at the river?"

He winks at me. "Not if we go down late at night."

I'm so relieved, I jump up and hug him. "Thanks, Denver."

He squeezes me back and rests his chin on my head. "Don't thank me yet." I giggle nervously, even though I shouldn't. "What's so funny now?"

"I can't believe you sent Gabi that Snap."

He steps back and takes my hand. "The trick is not letting her catch either of us alone. From now on, we stick together."

I let go of his hand. "We're partners in crime, Denver. That's it."

He gives me the once over, making me blush. "You sure about that, Ciara?"

I look away and bite my lip. "No, but I'm trying."

He lifts my car keys from my back pocket. "Come on, then. Let's go get the nets." My stomach knots. I have no idea who he's going to go see. He looks at me all business. "I meant what I said, Ciara. Until this thing is over, you stay close to me. I don't want you getting hurt."

I feel dumb feeling warmed by his words when he might just be the reason I'm in this trouble. I nod my head. "Let's go."

12

Denver drives my car, and we head out of town. Pretty soon we're on dirt roads. Just when I think we can go no farther, we round the bend to find an old farmhouse that looks abandoned. I wonder if this is his house, but I don't say anything. He pulls up in an empty driveway. I don't know what to do so I stay put. He walks a few steps before turning back to motion me to follow him.

I get out and hurry to his side. It's getting dark and we're out in the middle of nowhere. I stay close as we walk past a pond to a leaning shed with chipped, dull red paint that looks like a light wind could blow it down. I stand back as he pries open the squeaky door. He takes my hand and pulls me into the dark. He shuts the door before turning on his phone's light that he holds low and pointed at the ground. "Stay by the door." I do as he says. I grow more nervous by the minute, as he walks through outdated furniture of all shapes and sizes. It feels like we'll be here a while. I start to sit down. "Don't sit." I stand back up. "There might be mice in there."

I step away from the chair and try not to touch anything. He's clear in the back when I think I hear something outside. "Denver, someone might be coming," I whisper.

He shines his light on the floor. "Ciara. Get back here. Hurry!"

I stumble over a few things and try to be quiet. Right before I get to him, the door rattles. He shuts off his phone, grabs my hand, and jerks me to him. I body slam him. He touches my shoulder and pushes me down. We duck together as he pulls me back into a corner. The door flies open. "Damn door." There're footsteps and heavy breathing.

"Who's in here?" His voice sounds old and gravelly. I hear fear in his hitched breath. A bright light blinds me, and I look down. Denver scoots backwards quickly, and I do the same.

The light moves around the room in a sweeping motion. I see a pair of feet shuffling toward us. Denver picks up a bolt and chucks it across the shed. It hits something on the opposite wall. There's a loud clatter. The old man's flashlight aims in the direction of the noise. There's a flurry of movement as something skitters across the counter by the window. The man grabs a board and slams it down on the counter. I cover my mouth and hold back a gasp. "Damn animals. Get outta thar! Go on, get!"

He turns away. His light sweeps over us once more before he yanks open the door and slams it behind him. Denver holds my hand in his lap and buries his face in my neck. "That was close."

I grit my teeth, bump his chin with my shoulder, and sit still as long as I can stand it. "Can I get out now? I've probably got spiders up my shirt."

He wriggles out and tugs me up. "You want me to check?"

"No. Did you find your nets?"

He paws around on the counter I'm leaning on. "Yes."

I clear my throat. "Denver, who was that?"

There's a pause, followed by some heavy seconds. "My pops."

"How old is he?"

"I don't know. I met him after my mom took off."

"I'm sorry. I didn't know."

"Yeah, well. You're the only one who does know. At least round here." We walk across the grass. "The year I moved here, my mom and I showed up around midnight, and the next morning, she was gone."

I take his hand. "Did she ever come back to see you?"

He coughs. "Nope. She may have been on her way back, I don't know; but something happened to her, and she's never coming back now."

I squeeze his hand. "I'm sorry."

He shrugs his shoulders. "That's life I guess."

"Thanks for telling me."

He clears his throat. "I didn't tell anyone because I didn't want a pity party, you know?"

I nod my head. "Yeah. Sometimes I wish I lived in a place where not everyone knew my business all the time."

———

We get back to town late. He pulls down a side road that leads to the backside of the bridge. "Do you remember where you threw it?"

I sigh with frustration. "I try not to think about that day, Denver. I was just so scared."

"Maybe something will jog your memory when we get there."

I stare hopelessly out the window into the dark night. "Maybe."

He glances over at me. "You got booty shorts on?"

Where did that question come from? "Excuse me?"

"We're going river water wading, Ciara. You might want to take off those pants and shirt. Whatever you wear in there will smell rank when we're done."

I try to act cool about possibly stripping down in front of Denver, the most beautiful boy I know. "It's just like swimming, I guess."

We walk down to the rocks, and I try to look for any clues of where I was, but all I can think about is Denver in his boxers. No sooner do we reach the riverbank and he's dropping his shorts and tugging off his shirt. I look the other way. He laughs but doesn't move.

"Aren't you going in?" I plead. I really wish he'd go away.

"I can't. We have to carry this net a certain way or it won't work."

"Will you at least turn around?" All I can think of is how different I am from Gabi.

He shakes his head. "Nope. It doesn't matter anyway. I'll see the end result."

I glare at him. "I hate you so much right now."

I jerk my pants down before I rip off my shirt, and that's about the time I remember I'm wearing a red lacy bra and matching shorty shorts. I'm super embarrassed at Denver's stare, and I wish right now I did more sit ups in gym class. I can't take it anymore. I lean over to get the net. Denver coughs. "Stand up, Ciara. Don't move. I'll get it." His voice is hoarse, and his words sound strained.

I cross my arms underneath my chest. "Fine."

He stands up and hands me the net. "Here." He's acting all gentle and strange.

I snatch it from him. "Thanks." He just stands there staring. "What do we do now?"

He looks down at the net like he's never seen it before. "Right. We, um, we take it in the water."

"You said we have to hold it a certain way?"

"Oh, yeah." He backs up. His foot gets caught on something and he falls down. I hold out my hand, but he scoots backwards. "I've got it, Ciara. I'm fine. Don't touch me."

I step away, not knowing what to do next, and so I look out on the water and try to think of where I was when I dropped it. I look over and Denver hasn't moved. "Are you going to get up or sit there all night?"

He moves around and stands up. He keeps his distance. He gets in the water and walks forward. "Don't come in until I say." I wait on shore and watch as the big net unfolds itself. It takes a while, but it's finally stretched out as far as it'll go. "You can come in now."

I walk in barefooted, trying to ignore the disgusting feeling of the river bottom mud between my toes. I hate it. I walk slowly and try to get my bearings. It's strange to feel the weight of the net drifting under the water. I hope we don't catch a big snapper. "Don't think of snappers or snakes or..." I mutter.

"Stop it, Ciara!"

I turn to face Denver. "I'm sorry. I hate rivers."

"Just drag the net."

I think about this as we stumble along. The net grows heavier and heavier between us. "What good will that do? I mean, the only chance of finding it is if it's lodged under a rock or sitting on the bottom of the river, but if it's on the bottom of the river, will this net even catch it?"

I feel Denver's stare across the water. "I don't know. Do you have a better idea?"

I say the words that are in my head. "We could try to feel it with our bare feet."

He looks over at me. "That's not a bad idea. Don't let go of the net though."

I hold on to the net and walk around. I shuffle my feet in the disgusting mud as we walk in circles in the water. I look up in the dark night at the crescent moon. "Denver."

"Yeah."

"Where else have you lived?"

He clears his throat. "Why?" I don't like his tone.

"It's just a question. I'm making conversation."

"Oh. Where have you lived?" I make a face at him. "I asked you first, but that's an easy one. I've lived here my whole life."

He looks back at me, and we continue circling. "I think that's nice."

I hate the sadness in his voice. "I've lived in so many places, I stopped counting the number of schools after thirteen."

"Thirteen?" I can't imagine.

"Yep."

"Wow."

He snorts. "Traveling's not all it's cracked up to be."

"I guess not."

He's getting closer, so I move away. "You're tangling the net."

"You're tangling me." The intensity in his voice scares me, and I have to move away.

I think we're walking in the same place. I wander out farther until the water is at my chin. "Denver, why did you kiss me?"

"What kind of question is that?" He splashes water in my direction, and I could easily splash him back, and forget what I'm after, but I don't.

I need an answer to my question. "When I was twelve."

He turns away and walks out over my head. "You looked at me like you wanted *just me*, and I'd never had someone look at me like that before. I guess it was nice to feel wanted." His voice drops off, and I barely hear all the words.

I don't want to ask, but I want the answer. "Was I your first kiss?"

He turns back around to face me across the water. "Was I yours?"

My stomach churns. "I was twelve."

"I'm going to take that as a yes." I can't see his face in the dark, but I hear the smile in his tone.

I splash water at him. "Was I yours?"

He hesitates and looks up at the sky. I know the answer. My heart sinks a little in my chest. "You're the first one that mattered."

I giggle. "Good answer."

He splashes me again. "It's the truth." Oh, how I want to believe him.

I consider the water surrounding us. The river feels wide and impossible. "We could be out here all night and not find that stupid thing."

He slaps the water and sends out ripples. "I'm not ready to give up just yet."

I take a big step to broaden my search and go under. I'm sinking. I try not to panic as I come up. I kick my feet around like a maniac. I've never been a strong swimmer. Something slippery touches my foot, and I think I feel something. I surface. I want to holler out of fear and excitement, but I speak quietly. "Denver."

"Yeah?"

"Come here."

"What about the net?"

It's already weighing me down as I struggle to tread water with two legs and one free arm. "Just get over here."

He swims nearer to me, and I try to stay in place. I clumsily tread water. "I think I found something."

"What are you waiting for, Ciara? Get it."

It's getting harder to focus on staying in one place. My moving arm and legs are tired. "I can't. It's too deep."

"Well, where is it?"

I feel breathless as I try to answer. "I think it's right beneath me, under the water. I stepped in over my head and when I was coming back up, I think I stepped on it—maybe."

He swims closer. His legs brush mine beneath the water. "Move over." I doggy paddle awkwardly around him, dragging the net behind me. "Don't wrap that thing around me."

I almost go under again. I feel like an idiot as I crank my neck back to keep my head above water. "I gotta get to where I can stand. I'm not a good swimmer." Denver reaches out and grabs my arm and then my waist. He pulls me up against him and growls in my ear. "Just hold still and let me walk."

I keep a hold of the net. I feel like I'm going to sink him. "Denver, I don't think you should carry me and the net. I'm too..."

He leans back and turns his face to meet my lips. My free hand wraps around his waist. I pull away. My lips are slightly bruised, but I don't care. He's breathing hard. "You're perfect to me."

I'm so worked up I can't answer. This is madness. I'm in the middle of a dirty river, holding a fishing net, searching for drugs. This is the last place to start making out. "Did you feel anything?"

He chuckles. "Oh, yeah. I felt plenty."

I smack his chest. "With your feet, Denver. Did you feel anything that feels like a bag?"

He shuffles along. His jaw clenches. "There's no sidetracking you, is there, Ciara Yengst?"

I think he's trying to shame me, and this just ticks me off. "You don't get turned down much, do you?"

He stops moving. "What's that supposed to mean?"

76

"I just mean I bet most girls don't say no to you."

He looks away, shifting, and I think he's not going to answer, but then he does. "You're not most girls." His answer is muttered, and he sounds irritated, and I can't help but giggle.

"Nope. Just call me Nancy Drew."

He laughs at my answer, and I relax a little. "Do you know how many rocks and who knows what else I've stepped on tonight?"

I look around. I feel completely lost and disgusting as I can hear Char's chirping in my ear. "Do you have any idea how much bacteria is in river water?" I clap my hand over my mouth when I realize I was talking out loud.

He laughs. "Do you know how many ponds and lakes I've been in?" I smile at the thought of the boy I shared lemonade and brownies with splashing around in the summer sun. He wraps a leg around me, his foot slowly climbs, setting off new alarms, and I go still as a statue. "Enough to find this." His hand at my waist clamps on something and my hand follows, grabbing the bag. He grunts with the effort as he starts toward shore, all tangled up in the net.

I let go of him and step away as soon as my toe touches river bottom. We drag the net behind us slowly. I plop down on the shore and release the net to use both hands to untie the bag and empty it of rocks. I fish around and find the Ziplock bag. I yank it out. I'm satisfied when I feel a brick shape in my hands. I look over at Denver. "I can't believe you got it."

He's staring at me again. I must look like a drowned rat. "We make a great team." I freeze when I hear footsteps coming from the road. Denver jumps up and grabs our clothes. "Shit, Ciara. Run!"

The brick stays in my hand as I run for the trees. I feel as loud as an elephant, as leaves crunch and branches break beneath my feet. My heart races in my chest, and I don't know where to go or who is out here. As fast as I'm running, I'm picked up off the ground and shoved up against a tree.

Denver's body covers mine, and he whispers in my ear. "It might be nobody." I glare back at him as I clamp my hand over his mouth and shake my head.

I wiggle beneath him to scoot around and peek out from behind the tree. I spy two people down by the water's edge. "There's a net here." It's the man's voice from the video!

"So?" That's the old woman from the video! How'd she get out of the nursing home, and where is her wheelchair?

My eyes narrow. "How can The Neighbor be a doctor?" I whisper to myself.

"What?" Denver answers me before I can clamp my hand over his mouth, which I do anyway. Thank goodness the wind's blowing toward us.

"And it's wet. They could be close by." I can just imagine The Neighbor scanning the trees.

"I don't know. That net could have been here half the day. There's no way of telling."

The wind carries the voices I've come to know so well, and they sound like they're on the other side of the tree. I duck back behind in case they look our way.

"This is a tee shirt from the high school. I bet it's that girl from the barn."

The woman laughs, and chills run down my spine. "It could be anyone's tee shirt. This is a waste of time. Let's go." I listen as hard as I can. I pray their footsteps are headed back to the road and not into the woods.

I shiver with fear against the bark digging into my back as the breeze touches my wet skin. Terror consumes me. Denver's hands find my hips, and his lips meet mine. I lose a few seconds. I'm shocked at the feel of him, as my hands rove over him with a mind of their own before I come back to myself. I turn away and drop my hands. My cheek bumps the tree as I whisper, "Denver, please stop. We've got to get out of here." He rains kisses down my neck slowly, burying his face there, and I almost come undone, but my anger over losing my head when there's so much at stake and at Denver for exposing me wins out.

I shove him away and lean down quickly to grab his shirt. I throw it on and search around for my pants. I turn them right side out before jerking them on. I manage to find my shoes. I pick up the Ziplock bag I laid so carefully at the base of the tree. Denver grabs his shorts and shoes and stomps through the woods. I see the two of them before he does, I think. They're standing by my car, looking in the windows.

I rush after Denver, grab him by the back of his waistband, and then his arm. I yank him behind another tree, feeling desperate. I'm angry and frustrated, and Denver Evans is the reason. I shove him against a tree, meld my mouth to his, and skim his ribs with my fingertips. I don't let up until I feel his surrender. I glance sideways in the direction of my car. They're gone.

I unwrap myself and step backwards. "They're gone."

He leans back against the tree and stares at me. "What?"

I whisper, remembering the wind. "The man and woman by my car, they're gone."

He shakes his head. "Is that why you kissed me?"

I think of him and Gabi as I answer. "Does it matter?"

He sticks out his lip and I want to kiss him again. "What does that mean?"

I shrug. "Does it matter if it's me or Gabi, or somebody else you're kissing?" He knocks his head against the tree. I reach for his cheek, stop halfway there, and drop my hand. His pause ticks me off, and I answer my own question. "You can't answer my question, Denver. That tells me enough."

I start toward the car. "You got what you came here for, Ciara. That's all that matters to you." He mutters somewhere behind me.

We walk on in silence. I walk around to the passenger side as he climbs in the car, finding the keys beneath the driver's side floormat. "You left my car unlocked?"

"Would you rather I lose your keys by the river?" He growls. We back out. He turns around and heads back to town. He looks over at me. "Did you recognize the woman by the river?"

I hate that I can't read anything in his voice. "Did you?"

He sighs. "I asked you first."

I stick out my chin. "I asked you second." He doesn't answer. "It was dark. I couldn't see their faces."

"You could hear them, though."

"I don't know their names."

He snorts. "So you recognized their voices."

I smack his arm. "So did you! That was the man from the vi—from the barn."

He nods his head. "Oh, yeah."

I shake my head back and forth. "You're hiding something from me."

He glares back at me. "I could say the same."

I drop the bag on the floor, crying, because I'm spent. "I just want my brother to be safe, Denver. I'm doing this for him. You know that. This isn't who I am."

He pulls into the driveway and turns off my car. He stares out the front window. "What if it's who I am?"

I hate that I feel like Char as I answer. "Your life is only as hard you make it, Denver."

He wheels around to face me. "Sometimes we don't get to choose our lives, Ciara. It just happens."

I swallow hard and think of my parents. "You don't think I know that?"

Denver faces the front windshield again. "I'm sorry, Ciara. I wasn't thinking."

I look back at him, frustrated and furious. "Well start."

13

I grab the brick, take my keys, and head inside the house. I'm so ready for a shower, and so not ready to face school tomorrow, especially on four hours of sleep, as I glance at the clock that reads 3:30 a.m.

I wake up to an alarm clock, and as I lean over to my bedside table to shut it off, I discover Denver sleeping on my floor, about the same time Char sticks her head in. "What is he doing in your room?"

I look at her. "I don't know. I promise. He wasn't here when I fell asleep, but he must've slept there all night. I've got to get ready for school." She walks out and stomps down the stairs. I turn on Denver and glare down at him. "We don't have to stay together at night."

He turns over, stretches his arm out over my carpet, and tickles my toes that hang over the side of my bed. "I couldn't sleep." I can't stay mad at him when he looks up at me with his adorable bedhead, half-lidded hazel eyes, and sleepy smile. "You relax me."

I can't answer that, as he has the opposite effect on me, just as much this morning as any other time of the day. I take off down the stairs to make Char's coffee. I'm embarrassed when she walks in on me, humming. "What happened to my grumpy bear sister, who isn't civil until ten in the morning?" She teases.

I glance over at her and push the button to start the coffee. "I have no idea what you're talking about."

I race back upstairs to take a shower, open the bathroom door, and shriek as I catch half of a hairy leg from behind the shower curtain. I slam the door shut, grab my clothes and towel. "Char, I'm using your shower." I'm in and out in five. I slap on deodorant and lotion and yank on my clothes. I walk out to the breakfast table and sit down to eat.

Char calls to me from the front door. "Don't be late for school! Love you."

I wave wildly like a maniac answering across the room. "Love you, too."

Denver steps into the kitchen. He's a mass of wet curls in his faded blue jeans, signature band tee, and blue Vans, smirking at me. "Aww, thanks. I love you too." My heart trips, and I duck into another bite of oatmeal and bananas, unable to answer. He goes for his cup of tea and milk and leans down to sniff the back of my neck as he walks by.

I swat at his face with the back of my hand. "Could you not?"

He sits down at the table across from me. "I love the way you smell."

I fidget in my chair, desperate to change the subject. "So, where are we hiding it?"

"Inside the spare tire in your trunk."

His automatic answer scares the heck out of me. "Gee. You thought of that really quickly."

He frowns at me. "Yeah, well. My life hasn't exactly been a bouquet of roses."

I consider this. "The trouble with your answer is if you know that hiding spot, I'd guess they do too."

He nods his head. "That's a very good point."

I sit here thinking. "I don't want it in the house, because I don't want anyone ransacking this place, and I don't want it found here."

He nods. "This is true, too."

I notice his cup of tea. "Aren't you hungry?"

He shrugs his shoulders. "I could eat something."

"You want some oatmeal?"

He makes a face. "I'm not an old man."

"There are pop tarts and cold cereal in the cupboard, but we've only got about ten-fifteen minutes so you'd better hurry up."

He ignores me, sits there, and twiddles his thumbs. "Where could we hide it that they wouldn't find it until we want them to…" He stares across the table at me. "Do you have a cellar?"

I shake my head. "No."

"What about a shelter space underneath your house?"

"No."

"What about an attic?"

"I just said I don't want it in my house." He's staring at my front. "Denver. Eyes up."

He shakes his head and gives me a grin I've never seen before, and it curls my toes. "I'm just remembering." I jump up and take my bowl to the sink. "Remembering one very red, very lacy bra." I wheel around. I'm glaring and furious, but Denver is unphased. He looks at my front again! "Are you wearing it now?"

I say nothing as I stomp past him and smack the back of his head. "Shut up about my bra. I didn't wear it for you. You weren't even supposed to see it."

He frowns for a second, looking worried. "Who was?"

I wheel around. My fists are clenched at my sides. "Me!" I clamp my mouth shut. I feel like an idiot screaming at him in my own living room as I run up the stairs. I hear another set right behind me.

I grab the brick from underneath my bed. I have the sudden urge to chuck it through a window as Denver steps back in my room. "I'm just thinking, Ciara. Who do we know who's home all day, who we can trust?"

I turn around, smiling. "Cary!" Our voices together make me laugh. "Jinx!"

We rush back downstairs, carrying our backpacks. I lock the house and we hop in the car and head over to Cary's. A short time later, we pull up in his driveway. I hop out. Cary smiles and waves at me, but as soon as Denver gets out the other side, Cary's smile turns into a frown.

I walk up with my backpack. "Hey, Cary. I've got a favor to ask."

"What? I'm afraid to ask."

"I kind of found something that I thought I lost."

Denver leans in, talking low. "She found the drugs in the river."

I elbow him hard. "Shut up."

Cary's eyes widen. "You have them with you? Right now?"

"I'm sorry to ask you, Cary, but I have no choice. I can't leave them in our home unsupervised, and I can't carry them around in my car or my bag."

He glares up at me. "What are you going to do with it?"

"I'm going to give it back to the dealer so Crash can come home."

He shakes his head, staring at me. "You think it's as simple as that?"

I swallow hard. "I hope so."

He glares at Denver. "What's he doing with you?"

Denver steps up, answering. "We work together. We're a team."

Cary spits on the floor by his foot. "I don't trust you."

Denver's jaw clenches. "The feeling's mutual."

I look at the two of them, confused. "Cary, will you do it for me, please?"

"Fine." I dig it out of my bag, hand it over to him, and glance at my watch.

"Shoot. Now we're late for school."

We arrive at school in minutes and walk into the building. Denver turns to me. "Maybe it'll be easier to avoid everyone this way."

I turn to him. "You mean Gabi?"

He shrugs his shoulders. "Sure."

I race into first hour and sit down in the back row. Here comes Denver right behind me, plopping down as the second bell rings. I glance over at him, smiling, until I look forward to see Amarra, Gabi's best friend, giving me the stink eye. I look down at my paper, whip open a notebook to write down the daily question off the board and remember the little white boxes.

I raise my hand to use the restroom, run down the hallway to check my locker for another box, and I'm not disappointed. I hate the excitement mixed with dread I feel as I toss it in my bag.

The school day goes by fine until lunch time. I rush over to sit by Ari, who's also sitting near Gabi, who sees me for the first time today. Her eyes go wide. I ignore Gabi's weird look and focus on Ari. "Hey, Ari. How's it going?"

She turns to me. "Ciara, I'm surprised to see you here so soon."

I glance around her to see Gabi, who goes white as a sheet, before she collapses and hits the floor. That's weird. There's a bunch of commotion as half the table gathers around her, waiting for her to wake up.

I look back at Ari and Raul, who are staring at me like I have two heads. "So soon?"

Raul nods as he spins his bag of potato chips on the lunch table. "Yeah, after Saturday night." I blink. He looks at me like I'm crazy. "In the barn." I blush as I remember my act.

I lean into Ari, whispering, "Not everything is at it appears."

Out of the corner of my eye, I see the janitor talking to someone new. His stance is familiar, but his face isn't. The man answers, and my stomach drops out. I'd recognize that voice anywhere. It's the doctor from the video!

I jump up and try not to hyperventilate, or I'll be the next one on the floor. The walls are closing in on me. I rush toward Denver, who's headed my way. I grab his arm and jerk him around. "Act natural and follow me out into the hallway." I whisper. Denver walks beside me. I try to breathe as we get to the corner trashcan. I dump his whole tray and mine before I grab his hand. "I need to leave. Now."

I rush to the exit door, and we run outside to the car. I tear out of the parking lot, not breathing easily until we're at the house. I run upstairs, anxious to get to my laptop. I shove the SD card in as I lay across my bed. "Denver, watch the window. I hope he didn't follow us."

Denver doesn't move. "Who, Ciara?"

I can't believe he doesn't get it. "The doctor!"

"Who's the doctor?" He looks confused.

"The Neighbor!"

He looks even more confused. "Should I know who the neighbor is?"

I hit play. "The doctor and the neighbor are the same person, Denver, and he's also the dealer."

Denver hits pause and lays a hand on my leg. "Ciara. I'm so lost. Are you telling me the dealer is a medical doctor, and he's also the Neighbor?"

I do a giant eye roll. "Yes."

"And he's also the dealer who was after Crash."

I nod again. "Yes."

Denver shakes his head. "This is some strange stuff."

I nod my head. "I know."

Denver laughs, and it's so out of place. "Man. When your brother steps in it, he really steps in it."

I punch him in the arm. "Shut up and watch with me. This is important."

Denver settles in beside me. "What are we watching?"

I'm impatient and panicked. "I don't know yet. Just be quiet." I hit play.

The room is dimly lit. A door closes. The man steps to the bedside of the sleeping old woman, whose eyes fly open. "It's you again. Your visits have become more frequent."

"There's been another body, the boy. Blood for money."

Denver hits pause. "They're talking about Crash."

I nod. "I know." I hit play.

The woman stares unflinchingly at the man's face. "How can you be sure?"

"I was there. I heard her cries, I saw her tears as he swung through the air." I fidget uncomfortably at his words.

"Still, I'm not certain. People do many things in desperation."

"I know what I saw. Besides, I always thought he was weak." I snort. This man doesn't know my brother.

"How much is the setback?"

"You said you'd loan the money to me."

She glares up at him. "That's before this happened. They took one of ours and we took one of theirs. It's done."

He grunts. "Fine. Don't give me the money. Everyone said you wouldn't give anything up until you're dead. It doesn't matter. I made my point."

The lady pounds her fist on the cover. "What point is that?"

"No one will mess with me now. It's a small town. You know how rumors fly."

She continues to stare at him. "Tread carefully. Too much fear is not good for product."

"I know what I'm doing. High anxiety will only work in my favor." The man's voice is full of arrogance.

The woman slowly turns her head to stare at a blank space in the corner. The man sits, waiting. Minutes drag by. The man gets up off the bed and walks off screen.

The woman's whispery voice cuts through the small, dark room. "Watch your step. A victory trail made of blood can be very slippery."

I hit the pause button. Denver flips on his side, staring at me. "Where did you get that?"

I look at him in surprise. "It wasn't you?"

"What? I don't even know what that is."

I study him a bit longer before answering. "These videos show up in my locker. They have been for the past week or two."

He stares right back. "Damn, Ciara. You really do know how to keep a secret."

I look away, afraid I'll break down. "I don't know who's leaving them there, or why. All I know is I keep getting them, and they're driving me crazy. I don't even know if the person giving them to me has seen them."

"Well, the guy in the video is the guy from the barn."

I sigh. "Yep. He was at our school today."

"What?"

"Yes. That's why I ran out of the lunchroom. I heard him talking to the janitor, and I finally saw his face."

Denver's eyes are huge. "You think that guy is going to start working at our school? Why?"

"So he can keep an eye on me. He either knows my face, or it's because of the tee shirt at the river. That has to be the reason." I think I might puke.

"What are you going to do?"

I flip onto my back. "I don't know." Tears sneak out of my eyes, and I let them. "I wish Crash were here. I could talk to him about this."

Denver reaches for my hand. "I'm here."

I take my hand back. "It's not the same." I look over at him, feeling unsure. "I don't even know what role you play in all of this. Why are you here?"

He jumps off the bed and rubs his hand down his face. His fists are clenched. "I'm here to help you, Ciara. To protect you."

I stand up and stare him down because I need to know. "Why?"

He breaks my gaze. He paces back and forth. "I can't tell you that."

My brain hurts from thinking so hard. "You can't tell me, or you won't?"

"It's for your own safety, Ciara. Can't you just accept that?"

A dam breaks inside of me, and I explode. "A drug dealer's after me. My brother is supposed to be dead. Half the school thinks I'm a slut, and I may or may not have the enemy living in my home! You can't tell me why you're here, or whose side you are on?"

He grabs a hold of me, pulls me close as I fight him, putting my hands on his chest between us. He leans down and whispers in my ear. "I'm not your enemy, Ciara, and you're not a slut. You're the bravest, most honorable person I know."

I lay my head on his chest and dig my chin into his sternum just a little as I speak into his shirt. "Why did you have to be Gabi's boyfriend?"

He rubs my back up and down. "Fixed dynamics."

I laugh. "You don't even know what that means."

He pinches the back of my neck. "Be nice. It sounded good."

The door flies open, and we both turn to see Char storming into the room. Denver jumps behind me.

Char's face is beet red. This isn't good. "What are you two doing home in the middle of a school day? It better not be what it looked like!"

"I kept it in my pants!" I want to sink through the floor in mortification at Denver's words.

Char keeps glaring, so I try. "Char, I found the drugs in the river. I took them to Cary's. I didn't want to keep them here. We went to school and then I saw the dealer today. I think he works at our school now. I flipped out a little, and we came home."

Denver's still standing behind me. "And Gabi fainted in the lunch-room because she thinks Crash is dead and she didn't expect to see Ciara at school today. And half the school thinks Ciara's a slut."

I hang my head. Char comes barreling at Denver, and I step in front of her. "Denver let Gabi think we're together because he thought it'd distract her from Crash's hanging, but it didn't."

Char's face goes white, and she sits down in a chair, bends over at the waist, and holds her head. "Crash hung himself. I don't understand. I just talked to him last night."

I kneel before her on the floor and squeeze her knees. "No, Char. He didn't. But Gabi, Ari, Denver, and Raul saw a fake hanging in a barn the other night that Crash, Cary, and I staged and so they thought he did."

Char's knuckles go white. "I'm gonna kill Cary."

I grab her hands. "No, you're not. It was my idea. I was trying to buy us time. The dealer wanted Crash to pay him three thousand dollars, but Crash doesn't have it. That's why Tom had to shoot the hitman."

She shakes her head back and forth. "Who's Tom?"

Denver speaks up. "Walkman."

Char looks back at me. "Why do you know all of this?"

I look down at the floor. "Crash stole Tom's Walkman as a prank. I found it in his apartment after Denver and I... Never mind. I found it in Crash's apartment in a duffel bag and I opened it, and that's when I found the pills. I thought Crash was using, so I freaked out and threw them in the river."

Char looks at me again. "How long have you known all this?"

"About two weeks."

She narrows her eyes at Denver. "Why does the school think you're a slut?"

Denver coughs. "I kind of snapped a photo of Ciara and I on the couch, fully clothed, and sent it to Gabi; and she took it and ran with it on social media."

Char looks back at me. "Are you okay?"

That's the question that breaks me. I bury my face in her knees and bawl for real like a sick heifer for what feels like way too long. She pats my back and strokes my hair. When I finally slow down to a hiccup, she clears her throat. "Alright, little sister. You've had your cry, now it's time to go to work."

"Char? Will you call the school for me?"

She pats my head. "Of course, dear sister. And then you're going to come to work with me."

"What?"

"Yep. I'm not leaving you alone with Mr. Sexy Pants, and I can't stay home from work. So, you're going with me." I can't believe she called Denver Mr. Sexy Pants. He'll never let me live that down.

This is so not fair. "I can't clean up people. I'm not a Certified Nurse Assistant or whatever, I'm not even trained."

"No, but you can do laundry. We've been short in the laundry room for a month now."

Denver coughs. "A month? How's anything get done?"

She glares at him. "Are you volunteering?"

He coughs. "No."

"Denver."

"Yes, Char."

"I'm glad you're here. You can watch the house to make sure we have no unwelcome visitors."

I grab her knee again. "Do you really think..."

She cuts me off. "The guy came to your school looking for you. That's pretty ballsy. Either he's in trouble or he took it way too personal. I don't want to find out."

I look down at my clothes. "What do I wear to work?"

"Shorts and a tee. That laundry room gets hot."

I grab my gym clothes from my bag and run to the bathroom to change. I hate to admit it, but I'm thankful Char's in charge again. I can't think anymore today.

14

Char honks the horn outside, and I race down the stairs. "I'm late to work, Ciara."

I look over at her. "How can you be late to work when you practically live there?"

She laughs. "I guess that's about right." She wipes a tear from her eye. "I can't believe you guys staged a hanging. That's insane."

I follow her inside and get the heebie jeebies. I've never liked nursing homes. "What do I do?"

She squeezes a little lady's hand in a wheelchair as we go by. "Hi, Ruby." Char turns back to me. All her sweetness is gone. "Try to stay out of the way and just do what you're told. I gotta stop at the nurse's station."

I smile. This is where all the gossip happens.

Char steps up. "Hey, Monique. What's up?"

The short nurse with long multi-colored dreads shakes her head back and forth as she throws her hands on her hips. "I can't believe this. They know if they don't show up to work, we're short staffed. It's not like I can pull a couple of CNA's out of my magical nurse's hat." She puts her fingertips on her temples, humming.

Char snorts. "Monique, don't start with that again."

Monique hums louder, with her eyes closed tight. "Shut it, Char. I may have crossed the threshold. I'm about to conjure some help out of thin air." Char claps her hands, and Monique's eyes fly wide open. She makes a hand gesture in Char's face. "I was this close."

Char shakes her head at Monique's theatrics. "I ain't got time to commit you to the psyche ward, Monique, so, knock it off. Why don't you take some of your dramatic energy and channel it into delegating our teamwork to providing awesome patient care while working short-handed."

Monique makes a face. "Why does this always fall on me?"

Char grins back at her. "You're the Charge Nurse, and you do it so well. The rest of us are just low-paid peons."

Tall and sturdy, Tammy slaps Monique on the shoulder, a little too hard. "Buck up, princess. Just tell us what to do, and we'll get 'er done."

Monique gives her a scowl. "Tammy, I ain't no princess. I clean up as much crap as the next person on my shift. I'm just saying it'd be nice if our CNA's cared enough to come to work every night. And what's with them both being gone on the same night? That's gotta be more than a coincidence. Is there a party going on?"

Tammy laughs out loud. "I'm just a hard-working farm girl who does all the heavy lifting around here. What would I know about a party? Char here's the one with younger siblings. Why don't you ask her?"

Char sighs and turns to me. "Ciara?"

I throw up my hands. "Don't look at me. Everyone knows I have a warden for a sister who keeps me tied to the front porch. No one's sendin' me any party invitations."

Tammy laughs out loud. "You're a funny one."

Char heads in the direction of a call light before turning back. "Any more word on that patient with the virus?"

My stomach drops. Monique answers. "No, but that doctor of hers sure is rude."

It can't be. She can't be here! My brain is on fire. If she were here, that would make perfect sense. Being in the same town helps her keep close tabs on everyone. But what is she doing here, and who is she?

"Ciara!"

"What?"

"I just told you what you'll be doing. Please try to listen."

"I'm sorry, Char."

I follow her down a long, quiet hallway. We reach the laundry room. "Crystal, this is my sister, Ciara. She's going to help you with laundry today." Char shoves me into the room and walks away.

"First, you gather all the linen from every room. You just take one of these long containers on wheels and toss everything in there.

When it's full, you bring it back here." Crystal instructs me in a bored voice.

"How will I know what is clean and what is dirty? I don't want to make extra work for you."

Crystal laughs. "Trust me, you'll know." She hands me a pair of gloves. "Here you go."

I put the gloves on and step out into the hallway. I freeze when I see a dark figure sneak out a door. The figure runs up the hallway and rounds a corner. Something's not right. I step out, yank the tall trashcan on wheels behind me, and start up the hall. I peek around into the dark room, and almost faint when I recognize the bed with the chess table beside it. The bed is empty! I know that woman was in here. I glance to the corner and spy her wheelchair.

I run to her closet and search for anything that might mean something. I hear someone in the hall. I close the closet door, grab a paper off the floor, and run back to the hall, winded. I grab the trashcan and walk up the long hallway along to room 201, next to the nurse's station, like Crystal told me to do. I glance down at the paper in my hand once I get in the light. It's a hundred-dollar bill! I shove it down in my pocket. I step inside a patient's room and head for the bathroom. The smell gets stronger. I spy the laundry basket and try not to gag as I transfer the dirty sheets to my container.

I'm almost out of the room when I hear a voice. "You're new here, aren't you?"

I turn to see a long-legged man in a cowboy hat and glasses sitting in a chair in the corner. "Yes."

He smiles at me from under his mustache. "I'm Dale."

I smile back. "Nice to meet you, Dale. I've got to get back to work." I walk out the door and go to the next room. It takes longer than I think to get down this hallway. I round the corner and start down another when I hear a man hollering. I rush to the doorway and peek in. A tall man with thick white hair lies in bed. He sees me.

"There's someone in the closet." He points across the room.

I shake my head at him and try to get him to be quiet by putting a finger to my lips. He gives me a smile and mimics my actions.

"Shut your damn mouth, Bruce-y. There's no one there." Another voice yells back at him.

"Now, Roberto, be nice. Bruce, why do you think there's someone in your closet?" The man's voice behind me is friendly. He sneaks by in his blue scrubs. "Pardon me, dear." He must be one of the staff.

"I saw her. She went in there." The tall man says again.

"Ow! I've got a pain in my butt," the other man's voice calls out.

"Roberto! Don't say butt!" Bruce yells again, shaking his finger.

"Do you want some Tylenol for the pain?" It's the staff again.

"I don't know. That probably won't help." Roberto's voice is low and growly.

"Roberto," the staff member addresses him again.

"What?"

"Do you want some Tylenol?"

"I done told you, that won't help! Now go on, get!"

The man walks by me again in his scrubs. He shakes his head, muttering. "Darn call lights never stop. No wonder I can't get anything done."

"What you doin' in here?" Bruce's voice is quieter. I peek back in. There's a tall, thin lady with her back to me.

She leans over Bruce's bed. "I'm hiding something." I tremble with fear as I recognize the voice from the video. Why does she look different, and what is she doing in their room?!

"What you hiding?"

"Money."

"What for?"

"I need it."

"You got money? I want some." That's Roberto's voice.

"It's not your money, Roberto!"

"It's not yours either, Bruce-y!"

"You willing to die for it?" The woman's words make me wince. I peek around again. The woman is no longer in sight! Where is she?

"What good is the money if I'm dead?" Roberto's growling again, but he has a point.

"My momma died. She went to heaven. You're not going to heaven. You're a devil woman." Bruce-y's talking again. He points at someone I can't see.

The woman laughs, and my insides turn cold. She's definitely the woman from the video and the lady by the river. I'll never forget that laugh. "Probably so. You remember that, and don't say a word." There's silence. "Just like that. You be good boys now."

"I'm a good boy." Bruce looks at me again. I run down the hall, hide in a closet. I shake as I hear light footsteps run by. I open the door, walk toward their room again, and step inside.

Roberto pipes up. "That damn crazy woman stole my damn money."

Bruce answers. "Where'd the pretty lady go?"

"Oh, shut up!" Roberto yells.

"That's not very nice."

"Shut up, I said!"

I look at Roberto. "Where'd she put the money, Roberto?"

He sneers at me. "Who are you?"

I step closer to him and try to smile, though I'm terrified she'll come back and find me here. "I'm trying to help you stay safe."

Bruce looks at me. "She put it up there."

I look at him. "Up where?"

He points to the corner, and I see a vent. "Up there. She put it up there."

I stand on the chair beneath the vent, but I'm not tall enough. I text Denver. I get back to work, but I can't shake the feeling that someone's watching me, like the first day of school. I rub my hand absentmindedly on the back of my neck as I try to walk faster down this long, dark hallway. I hate nursing homes.

I'm almost jogging with the cart stacked full of linen that I pull behind me. I'm about to round the corner and the wheels bump against my heels. I hear Char's muffled voice. I glance back at the vented door I just passed. I back up slowly. "Cary, I need her here. I don't want her going in the jail with you."

I don't care what they're talking about, I'm going. "Char, she's the one who's been putting all the pieces together. I need her with me." I stop at Cary's voice. What's he doing here?

I can't believe Cary's words. I flush at his praise. "Cary, promise me you'll watch out for her."

He laughs. "Your little sister can watch out for herself."

"Promise me." I want to cry at the tone of Char's voice.

"Ouch. Alright, I promise."

There are breathing sounds and other things. Ew. I clear my throat as I come around the corner. "I'm ready to go."

She eyes the linen cart. "You're just going to leave it there?"

I look down the long hallway and remember the eyes on the back of my neck. "Yep. Come on, Cary. Time's a wastin'."

15

Cary talks as we bump along in his Ranger. "I don't know if seeing Walkman in lock-up is the best idea, but I don't know how else to get a hold of the main man."

I shudder at the thought. "Yeah."

We pull into the parking lot, and I follow Cary inside. He scribbles down Tom Edwards on the paper at the window. He turns to me. "I wonder if Denver's seen his cousin Tom lately." My stomach drops out, and I take a deep breath. Cary glances over at me. "Ciara, are you okay?"

"Huh? I just don't like prisons." No, I'm not okay. Tom 'Walkman' Edwards and Denver Evans are related. I feel so stupid! That's why Denver's here. To protect his cousin or brother, or whatever they are to each other, which is why I'm here, to protect my brother. "Focus."

Cary laughs beside me. "So the muttering isn't just a Char thing."

I swat at his stomach. "Shut up, Cary."

Walkman shuffles out. His hands and feet are shackled. He sits down at the table across from us, with his telltale goofy grin in place. Cary's jaw clenches. "You can drop the act now, Walkman. I know who you really are."

Walkman just keeps grinning, and cocks his head to the side. "Do you? Does it matter who I am? Maybe I'm just happy to be free."

Cary snorts beside me. "Look at your hands and feet! You're not free!"

Walkman's smile falters a little. "I'm free from my responsibilities. The landlord can't follow me in here, and neither can my grandma."

Cary leans in. "Walkman, I need a favor. I need…"

Walkman cuts him off, laughing. "I already did you a favor, Cary; a huge one. I killed Jimmy."

Cary glares back at Walkman. "Keep your voice down! That was self-defense. And no one ever asked you to kill anyone. You know that."

Walkman shrugs his shoulders. "Doesn't matter, man. Jimmy's gone, and you don't have to worry about him, so I'd say we're more than even."

Cary keeps staring at Tom. "I need a name and a number, Walkman, and you're going to give them to me. I need to be able to get a hold of the neighbor. I don't want to wait around like a sitting duck, waiting for him to get the jump on me."

Walkman leans back in his chair, looking all smug. "If you want to see your neighbor, just go knock on his door."

I hold back a laugh. Cary slams a hand on the table so hard, he almost knocks it over. "Don't play cute with me, Tom. Give me the number for the dealer."

Tom smirks. "I don't have it. All I've got is a dead man's phone number. And that won't be of any use to you."

I've about had it. I lean forward. "Tom, if it doesn't matter, then just give it to us."

He winks at me. "Hey, little birdie. What are you doin' here? Shouldn't you be out with my cousin, your hunk-a-hunk of burnin' love?" I blush at the thought.

Cary pounds the table. "Stop messin' around, Walkman. I need that number."

Walkman talks low. "Slip me a piece of paper."

Cary gives him a piece of paper and a pen. Walkman writes it down quickly and slips the paper back across the table.

Cary holds out his hand. "Give me back my pen."

Walkman's hands are empty when he lays them down, still shackled. "What pen?"

My unease has risen by the minute since we stepped foot inside the jail. I don't even like Tom. I don't know why I'm asking. "Are they treating you alright, then?"

Walkman's strange smile is back. "Yep. Turns out I'm kind of a celebrity for killing off Jimmy. Guess he had a lot of enemies."

I don't know what to say. "Well, I guess that's good then. I think I'll take off. Is there anything you need?"

Walkman looks back at us, winking. "Nah, I'm good. I've got everything I need now. This Jailhouse Rock gig ain't so bad."

He goes to get up, but I remember the list of names. "Walkman, what did Denver want?"

"He came by to say hello, to see how I was doing."

Cary's not in the mood for games as he grips Walkman's hand hard. "What did he want? Don't play dumb with me."

Walkman remains unphased, wiggles his hand away, and taps his fingers on the table. He glances all around the room, hunches over, and raises his eyebrows. "Don't you all have cameras rollin' all the time? Why you need to know?"

I try again. "Walkman, I know you like games, but this isn't a game. People's lives may be in danger! Why did Denver come to see you?"

Walkman side eyes me. "You should know, *Ace Detective*. He just stopped by to catch up on old *family* news."

I keep my face blank. Tom wants a reaction and I'm not giving him one.

Cary leans forward. "Walkman, tell me what Denver was after."

Walkman sets his hands on the table and leans back in his chair. "What do you have for me? I already gave you a number. You want more than that, you gotta give me something."

Cary reaches into his jacket pocket and lays a pack of cigarettes on the table. Walkman looks unimpressed. "Is that all you've got? I was hoping for a case."

Cary pffts and opens his jacket wide. "That's all I've got. Some of us have to *pay* for our meals."

Walkman pockets the cigarettes. "He wanted a number, just like you, except he wanted someone else's."

Cary's face is confused. "Whose number?"

Walkman cocks his head. "*That* is the million-dollar question."

Cary glares at him. "Did you give him anything?"

They sit in silence, staring each other down. Walkman glances around. He looks like he has a delicious secret, like he's been waiting all day to say his next words. He gets up slow and easy, stretching as much as possible in his shackles, and enjoying every bit of irritation written all over Cary's face. He starts to walk away, turns back to Cary like an afterthought, and flips the pen across the table. "I gave him The Neighbor's number."

Cary explodes and jumps out of his chair, yelling. "Who's the Neighbor?"

Tom's expression remains blank as he looks up at Cary, who stands beside me, shaking and angry. Tom smiles as he speaks. "Mr. Rogers."

I struggle to hold back laughter as Cary breathes hard beside me.

We watch Walkman walk away, shuffling through the double doors, bopping his head to an imaginary beat.

Cary takes a deep breath before calling out. "The jig is up, Walkman. We found your mother."

Walkman stops and spins around. A trace of emotion crosses his face before he goes all chill again, as he answers Cary with his hands out in front of him, palms up, empty-handed. "I'm left, you're right, she's gone." He spins around and walks away once more, but his steps are slower, and his imaginary bopping beat is gone.

Cary shakes his head, muttering as he walks out. "He's the most infuriating... He must be working on an insanity plea." He walks a few steps and stops again. He turns to me. "Do you know a Mr. Rogers?"

We walk out. My mind remains elsewhere. I'm about to explode with the revelation of Tom and Denver being related. "Cary, drop me by the house."

Cary looks nervous. "But Char told me to take you back to work."

I grab his arm. "This is more important than work. I need to talk to Denver, and I need to do it now!"

He sighs. "Fine."

I turn back to him. "Mr. Rogers was a kid's T.V. show."

He stops in his tracks. "What?"

"You know, the guy who wore the cardigan sweater and he was everybody's friend?"

Cary smacks his forehead. "Ugh. I hate Tom's riddling."

We hop in the car and soon we're at the house. Cary goes to get out, but I put a hand on his arm. "Could you just wait here, please? I think it'll go better if you do."

Cary shrugs. "Happy to. I don't want to talk to Denver anyway."

I get out to run inside. I'm ready for an epic showdown as I unlock the front door and slam it shut. I'm surprised to see Denver fast asleep on the couch. I walk over to him and shake his shoulder. "Wake up, Denver Evans." He reaches for my legs and wraps his hand around the back of my knee, a feeling I didn't know I loved until now. I swat his hand away. "We've got things to talk about. No funny business."

He looks up at me in surprise by the sharpness of my tone. "Should I know why I'm in trouble?"

He sits up slowly. His sleepy eyes make me feel all kinds of warm as I stand here with my arms crossed. "Denver, when were you going to tell me you're related to Tom?"

He looks at me funny. "You didn't know?"

I plop down at the end of the couch, trying to decide if I believe him, which I hate. "No, I didn't know. His last name is Edwards, and yours is Evans."

He looks uncertain as he looks back at me. "We're first cousins. Our moms are sisters. It's a long story."

I don't drop my stare. "Indulge me."

"I will, but could you maybe tone down your hostility?"

I shrug my shoulders. "This is news to me, and a huge piece of the equation." My head hurts from chasing after pieces I didn't know were missing. "I'm still deciding."

He tries to look out the window from the couch, but the curtains are drawn. "Is someone in the driveway?"

I glare back at him. His stalling tactics are so irritating. "It's Cary. He's waiting on me. Should I invite him in?"

He glares back at me. "No."

"Why do you two..." I stop. "You know what? That's for another time. I need the story." I tap my foot in annoyance. "Now."

He stares at the floor. "Fine. I'll tell you, but you can't interrupt."

I shake my head. "I won't." I wait. "Just quit stalling."

"I'm not, I'm just trying to..."

I slap the couch. "Start at the beginning! That's how most stories go."

"Alright, already! As I said, my mom was Tom's mom's sister. They were never close, but when they were together, it was creepy. Even as a little kid, I hated to be around my Aunt Elle, because she was always hiding something. I don't even know if that is her real name. We didn't see her much, but when we did, my mom and her would always be in a corner, whispering. And everything she said was like a riddle. It was like talking to the Joker."

He stops. A lightbulb goes off inside my head "Like Tom. That's why he talks in riddles."

He nods his head. "Makes sense. I never thought about it." I give him an incredulous look. "I've got my own baggage weighing me down, alright?" His voice is all defensive.

"Fine. Go on."

"So, one time when my aunt came to visit, my mom left with her, I think. And that's the last time I saw my mother."

"But you said your mom left you at your dad's house."

He sighs. "She did. But someone came to get her. I know they did, because she was gone in the morning, but her car was still at my dad's."

Wait. What? "Where is that car now?"

He shrugs. "It's probably still at my dad's place."

"We need to go through it! It could have a clue." I stop Denver when he gets up. "Wait. What's the rest of the story?"

He sits back down. "After my mom left, my dad got a phone call a few days later. I wasn't supposed to be in the house, but I had been hanging around, waiting for her to come back. I felt like he was hiding something from me. I listened in because my dad never got phone calls." He stops talking. I wait him out. "I heard him say 'It's done. We're settled now.'" He swallows hard. "About a month later, my dad's eyesight got much worse, and then his mind just went."

I squeeze his hand. "I'm so sorry, Denver. What do you think happened?"

He looks back at me. His eyes are filled with a darkness I've never seen in him before. "My Aunt Elle happened. I think she killed my mom. I think she's got a trail of bodies behind her that no one's ever found."

I sit back, stunned. "So, this mess is bigger than the drugs, and your aunt might be a serial killer, and you think she's tied up in what we're in."

He looks back at me. "Yeah. And if I know her like I think I do, that wrapped up brick is just the tip of the iceberg."

A car honks outside. "Does Cary know?"

He frowns. "I didn't tell him."

I hate feeling helpless. "We need a plan."

"What?"

"Obviously, your dad knows something that he's not telling, and it has to be big."

"What do you think he knows?" Denver sounds worried, but he also sounds like he's afraid I'll find out something he doesn't want me to know, but I can't stop now.

"He owed your aunt something, or she was holding something over his head. It *has* to be that." I swallow hard. "We have to go back to your dad's place."

He shakes his head. "That's a terrible idea, Ciara."

I grab his hand. "Denver, it's the only one I've got." The car honks again, and I run outside. "Cary, tell Char I can't come back. I'll be gone for a few days. Denver and I have work to do."

He jumps out of the car. "Ciara, this is a horrible idea."

I have to make him see. "Cary, it's the only choice we have. I'm close to the answer. I can feel it. I know I can figure this out. I have to, before they find us." I remember the woman in the hall. "And Cary, stay close to Char. There's danger at her job."

His eyes are huge. "What?"

I step closer, talking low. "I believe Tom's mom is hiding out in the nursing home as a patient, but she doesn't know that we know she's there. The drug-dealing neighbor just got a job at our high school. I think he's looking for me because he's figured out I'm Crash's sister because of the night at the barn. I have to get away and I have to break this case before he gets to me." I grab Cary's arm. "He's been in-and-out of the nursing home, talking to the mysterious old woman."

Cary studies me for a while longer. "Ciara."

"Yeah."

"Be careful." He hugs me tight, and it's too much. I wish so much my dad was here right now, and for a little while, I forget it's Cary I'm hugging. I step back. I'm embarrassed by the tears on my face. "Thanks."

16

I run back into the house. "Denver, we're going on a road trip."

"I'm sorry, what?"

"Cary knows what I need him to know to keep Char safe. You and I are going to figure this thing out."

He jumps up, looking all nervous. "Just like that?"

I nod my head, getting more excited. "Yep. Just like that."

He stands in front of me, holding my hands in his. "Are you sure?"

I shake my head. "No. But I'm not walking those creepy dark hallways anymore."

"What?"

"Golden Ages ain't so golden."

He picks me up off the ground and spins me around. "Ciara Onxy Yengst. You are the bomb!"

All these secrets are getting to me, and I feel like I'm going to explode if I don't put an end to them. "I'm a bomb alright." He's still spinning. "You want me to puke on you?" He stops spinning and puts me down. "We need money, groceries, chargers, and a flashlight."

He reaches under the couch cushion and pulls something out. "And a gun."

I flinch. "Whose gun is that?"

"Your brother told me where to find one before he left."

I can't believe I'm asking this. "Is it loaded?"

He yanks it back, and I can't help but think his hands look awfully comfortable holding the gun. He looks up, smiling. "Locked and loaded."

I glare at him. "For the record, I hate guns."

He sticks his tongue out at me. "God bless the second amendment." His exaggerated Southern twang almost makes me laugh out loud, but it stops at my lips because I can't take my eyes off the gun.

I march past him into the kitchen and grab a paper bag as I talk to myself. "Pop tarts. Loaf of bread. Peanut butter. Honey. Bag of chips. A few clothespins. Cooler of water bottles."

He makes a face. "Honey?"

I wink at him, feeling bossy. "Honey doesn't go in the fridge. Jelly does."

He winks back. "You're a keeper."

I study him a second before looking down. I wish it were that easy. I open the cookie jar. I'm surprised that I almost forgot. I count out $142.00. "Dang it. This will be cutting it close."

He looks over at me. "You need money? I know where to find that."

I hate my lack of confidence in him. "Denver, you live on street corners half the time. Where are you going to find money?"

He shrugs, looking down. "So, I live on the fly. Maybe I like it. I've got money. I just don't spend it."

"Okay, I'm sorry. Where are we going?"

He looks back at me. "You going to wear those clothes for the next three days? I mean, I don't mind, but you might."

I smack my head. "Clothes!" I go running up the stairs.

"Don't forget to pack that red bra!" He yells after me. He's never going to let me live that down.

I almost trip as I answer. "Shut up."

I grab a bag and start stuffing. Underwear, tees, sweats. I close my eyes as I stuff my red bra in the corner of the bag. I run to the bathroom, grab my shower bag, and drop soap and shampoo in. I grab a few rolls of toilet paper. I glance in the mirror and hardly recognize myself. "Ciara, what are you doing?" I whisper. The mirror provides no answers.

I run back down the stairs. "What about you? Where's your clothes?"

He picks up his school backpack. "Right here."

We grab all the stuff and head for the car. I hold up my pinkie, feeling like I'm violating mine and Crash's sacred tradition, but he's not here, and I need a boost of confidence. "Pinkie promise?"

Denver looks at me like I'm nuts. "Excuse me?"

"Just shake pinkies with me." He wraps his pinkie around mine, and I squeeze. "Backs to the wall 'til the last man falls." I push his hand up 'til it touches the car ceiling. I kiss my thumb on the way down and drop my hand.

"What's that mean?"

I shrug. "I don't know. Crash came up with it. He used it mostly to get psyched for wrestling."

He chuckles. "I'm guessin' he didn't use the word 'back'."

I turn red. "Well, I'm a girl, so we kind of had to change the words." I turn on the ignition. "Where to, Denver?" He looks at me, questioning. I stare right back. "Show me the money."

"Oh, yeah. Well, you said we had to go back to my dad's house."

I back out. "Please tell me we're going to the shed and not your father's house."

He nods. "Yep."

I think about this on the way. "How many doors are on his house?"

"Why?"

"I think we should block them from the outside to buy us time to search the shed."

"You want to barricade my dad in his home?"

"We'll take them out before we go."

"Fine. What are we looking for?"

I tap the steering wheel. "I don't know yet. I'll know it when I see it." I say with more confidence than I feel.

We get to his house. I wait in the car while Denver sneaks up on his dad's place. Soon enough, he's back to the car and we're heading for the shed.

It's a little less creepy in the daytime, but after about an hour of looking through piles and piles of stacked up things filling every corner of every space, I'm frustrated as ever as I stand in the back corner beside a chair big enough to be a throne. I know what Denver said about mice, but I don't care anymore. I plop down on it. I watch Denver methodically go over everything, and I feel defeated. I was so sure something would speak to me, but nothing has. He must feel my stare as he turns around. His eyes narrow as they fall on me. "Get off that chair." His command is so serious.

I throw up my hands. "I'm too tired to be afraid of a few mice."

He shakes his head. "No, that's not why. It's just that's my dad's chair. He never let anyone sit on it or touch it. Ever. I can't believe he put it out here. Get up, please." An idea comes to me, and I stand up. I run my hands carefully over the chair. "What are you doing?"

I look back at him. "If anything is in this shed, I'd bet it's in this chair."

He walks over to me. "Really?"

"Think about it. Why do you think he didn't want you touching his chair?"

I feel all down the back of it. I find lumps about ¾ way down. "Bingo. You got that pocketknife?"

He glares at me. "I'm doing the cutting."

I step back. "Be my guest but cut up above. You don't want to damage the money. I guarantee you that's what's in here."

Denver cuts into the fabric at the top of the chair. I peel it back. My eyes bug as I reach down and pull out bricks of cash. "Ho-ly crap." He grabs a canvas backpack off the floor. I watch it for movement. "Check that thing for rats. I don't want them in the money." He turns it inside out and shakes it good. We fill the bag, but I hesitate. I put one back. "Your dad might need it someday." My hand brushes on something else as I go to shove the money down deep in the chair. I pull it out. It's an old wedding picture. I turn it over, but there's no writing. I hand it to Denver.

He holds it up in the light. "That's my mom and my aunt, and that must be my aunt's husband. I didn't know she was married."

I take it back and study the man. "That has to be Tom's father. I can see the resemblance."

"He's dead, you know." His voice is all quiet again.

"Who?"

"Tom's father. He was murdered. She was there."

I shudder again. "Did she do it?"

He shrugs his shoulders. "She said she didn't. She said she shot the man who shot him, but who knows? She might have shot them both."

"Denver! What a thing to say."

He looks at me again. "I'm telling you, she's worse than awful. You don't know. One time my mom was arguing with her on the phone and my mom said, 'You going to burn my house down, too?', and then she hung up the phone."

I shake my head. "How's a woman like that get away with all of this?"

He puts the picture in our money bag. "That's why we have to catch her."

I look down at the money. "Do you suppose these are marked bills?"

"What?"

I catch my breath. "Is there any chance your aunt robbed a bank?" I think hard. "This money could be evidence. Maybe that's why your dad kept it."

He sits down. "I never thought of that."

We sit for a few minutes. "Denver, where's your mom's car?"

"You still think there's something in it?"

"I don't know, but we've got to find some way to pin all of this on your aunt, and the man." I fidget. "She's gotta go down for something. She's never going to stop chasing us."

He looks through the windows toward the house. "Right now, we gotta get out of here. Dad must have heard our car pull up, because he can't see anything."

I hear gun fire outside. "You bastards! I told you not to come back!" The old man hollers as he strides awkwardly across his lawn with his shot gun.

Denver pushes against the back door to the shed with his shoulder, but it doesn't budge. "Hurry, Denver!" Another shot fires outside.

He puts the bag down and runs at the door. It gives a little, but not near enough. He rears back and kicks the doorknob, hollering out. The whole door flies off! He's so hot. He grabs the bag of cash. "Ciara, go!"

I sprint out in front of him, and we take off through the grass. We run around the opposite side of the shed. By the time I get to the car, I'm winded. We hop in and take off down the road. "Think, Denver. The car's important."

"I'm trying."

"Was there a place your mom loved, or a place that was special to her?" I feel bad for asking him to go down memory lane, as it's a place I try to avoid because it hurts too much.

"She used to talk a lot about this ghost town, how it had a bread store and a post office, and she and Elle would play in them sometimes."

"Was there anything specific she had a fixation with?"

"I don't know."

"Where is this town?"

"It's like four hours from here. Do you really think there's something there?"

"I think it's a start."

I get a text from Ari. That's weird. She never texts. She only Snaps. I go to open it. Denver snatches my phone.

"No texting and driving."

"I'm not texting. I was reading."

He opens my message and starts reading it aloud. "How's DD?" He stops and smiles over at me. "Am I DD?"

I'm angry and flustered. "Yes. What's the rest of the message?"

"What's it stand for?"

"I'm not telling you. Just tell me what she says."

He holds my phone in his hands, turning it over, and annoying me on purpose. "I don't think I will."

"Denver, come on. It might be important."

He rolls down the window and holds my phone in the wind. "Tell me, Ciara."

I lunge for my phone. The car swerves across the gravel. He reaches out and grabs the wheel. I look over. His other hand is empty. "You dropped my phone!"

I slam on the brakes. He pulls it out of the seat and holds it up. I snatch it back from him. "That's not funny."

"Damn, you're a stubborn woman."

I open the message from Ari. "How's DD? Something weird happened today. A true crime writer showed up at the school office looking for you! I know because I was in the office during my T.A. hour. I was at the copying machine for Mr. B. We're starting matchbox cars again."

I text her back. "Was it Alex Smith?"

"Yes! How'd you know?"

A balloon of happiness swells up inside of me. "I e-mailed him on a hunch."

Ari sends me a GIF of a man shaking his head with his palms up. "I don't want to know."

I lay the phone down, smile from ear to ear, and ignore Denver's staring. "What is it now?"

I turn to him. "Another piece of the puzzle."

I put the car in drive and hit the gas. "Which is?"

I laugh. "I don't know, DD."

He reaches over, squeezes my leg, and moves his hand slowly upward. My face flames. I grab his hand and move it. "Don't do that."

He leans over and breathes in my ear. "Do what?"

I shove him hard. "Denver, I'm warning you." He reaches over, strokes the back of my neck, and plays with my earlobe. "Please stop." He drops his hand, and I feel cold. "I e-mailed a true crime author and gave him generic details on this story, and I heard back from him."

"And?"

"Well, he thinks he might know who Tom's mom is."

"Really?" He sounds so surprised.

"It's a long shot, but he told me he grew up next to a girl who burned her grandma's house down, and then she left town, but not before her husband died and she shot someone."

He slaps the dash. "No way! That's got to be Aunt Elle."

"Apparently, this guy's a writer and he's written a few books, but the story he's always chased after was your aunt's story. The only weird thing is, he never mentioned she had a sister."

Denver shrugs. "That's not a big deal, really. I mean, maybe he forgot about my mom because Aunt Elle is so noticeable. She has a way of taking up a lot of space."

I mutter to myself. "And leaving a lot of empty space behind."

He stares out the window. "That too." He answers so quietly and seriously, I feel a little bad about what I said.

We drive on in silence. He coughs. "Seriously; when are you going to tell me what DD stands for? Is it Dangerous Denver, or Daring Denver, or..." He throws his hands up. "That's all I've got." I swallow hard. I can't believe I told Ari the nickname I gave him. His eyes bore into the side of my head, but I keep my mouth shut. He slaps his knees. "My turn to drive."

I whip my head sideways. "Why?"

He grins at me. "I'm bored, and I'm just going to keep bugging you about the name if you don't let me drive."

I consider this, and the fact that if I'm not driving, I can be on my phone and troubleshoot in my notebook. "Alright, fine." I pull over on the side of the road that's in the middle of nowhere.

I barely stop the car, and he's at my door. He opens it and grabs my hand to pull me out and flush up against him. I know what's coming, but I don't stop it. His kiss is so hot I barely feel the burn of the hot car door on the small of my back, as his hand heads South. That registers. I shove him backwards. "What the hell, Denver?"

He steps back toward me, not looking a bit sorry, as his hand rests at the base of my neck. His fingertips brush over my pulse. "What's it stand for?"

I would laugh if I wasn't so worked up, but I'm also ticked off that I just got played. "Dumb Denver."

His hand drops, and he grabs the keys from my hand. He looks sucker punched, and I feel like an awful person as he climbs inside wordlessly. I stand here, not knowing what to do. He stares straight ahead. "You going to get in the car, or should I just leave your ass?"

My eyes water, and I can't believe the feeling of triumph I have over his look of defeat. I look at him again, trying to decide if he's for real, because the Denver I know never lets anyone crack his walls.

I walk around the back of the car and climb into the passenger side. We ride on in silence. I reach for the radio, but he swats my hand away. I try to focus on writing down theories, but nothing comes to mind. I pick up my phone for inspiration, but all I can see is the DD in Ari's text and the clenching of his jaw, as it gets tighter and tighter. "Stop the car!" He slams on the brakes, and I flinch. "We've got to stop doing that or we'll have no tire tread left."

I can't believe what I'm doing as he turns to me. I get up on my knees, lean over to kiss his jawline, which leads me to his lips, but he remains still as a statue, and so I whisper the truth in his ear. "Delicious. Delicious Denver." My insides turn to molten lava, and I ease away from him, heading back to my side of the car.

He frames my face, whispering, "You're so hot." He plants another on me, and I let myself get lost for a little while, but then I hear Char's words in my head, and I pull away. "We've got to get going."

He looks at me all frustrated. "Can you really just turn it off and on like that?"

If only he knew. "I don't know. I've got a lot of things on my mind."

"You're driving me crazy over here, Ciara. You know that?"

I smile a little as I stare out the window, because if I keep looking at him, this car's going to be parked in the middle of the road for a very long time. "Just drive."

He grabs my hand, and I pull it away. "That's all I get?"

This is the Denver I can handle, the one that gets under my skin. I turn on him. "Yes, Denver. That's all you get. Quit your whining. You just want sex, and I'm not giving it to you."

He coughs. "That's not all I want."

I cross my arms. My eyes going wide. "Oh, really? And just where did you think this was going to end?"

"I don't know."

I feel like a nun. "Well, I do. I'm not here for that. We're here to solve a mystery. You got your answer from me. So just be happy with that."

He pouts like a little boy as he starts back down the road, muttering, "You didn't have to go all vixen on me, whispering in my ear." My face flames red again, and I reach for the radio. I crank it up to drown him out, but fate is against me at the moment, when he starts singing along with the radio. "If I said you had a beautiful body, would you hold it against me…"

I change the station, and he laughs out loud. I turn it off. "This is important. What could your mom have that your aunt didn't want her to have?"

"I have no idea, but I know my mom was afraid of her. She was always talking about insurance."

I snap my fingers. "She had something on your mother!"

He shakes his head. "No. Like car insurance. See, mom had this one bag, and her boyfriend, Dick." He stops and shakes his head. "His name fit him so well."

I smack his arm. "Go on. What about the bag?"

"She had some bag and Dick was always giving her crap about taking that car book with her everywhere. She would always say it's where she kept her mileage notes."

I shake my head. "But she didn't keep it in the car?"

"No."

"Did you ever see her write in it?"

"No."

"It has to be a diary or something like that. I bet it's something that your aunt wrote, and your mom took it because she thought it would keep her safe."

He stares at me. "Ciara, you're a little creepy."

I make a face at him. "I'd like to think I'm intuitive."

He shrugs. "That does sound better." I glance over at Denver. His long legs fill up my driver's side. His big hands cover half my wheel. His easy-going manner (most of the time) washes over me like a cool breeze. I'm in big trouble. He side eyes me. "What you thinking?"

I look away and stick my hand out the window. I watch the crops lean in the wind. "I'm thinking I like the quiet, and the cool air that blows through my fingers as the wind grazes the tops of the dandelions in the field." I turn back to him. "That's all."

He takes my hand in his. "That's real nice." His voice lowers. "I was thinking about you."

I leave my hand in his. "I was thinking about you, too."

He grazes my thumb with his. "Did you leave me with the dandelions?"

My heart skips a beat and I look back at him in surprise, giggling. "Maybe."

17

My phone Facetimes. It's Cary. I open it. "Hey, what's up?"

He stares at me. "*You've* been getting the flash-drive videos?"

"*You're* the one sending them?"

"Yes, I thought they were getting to your brother, but apparently not. I had him listen to this last one, and he freaked out a little before he told me he'd never heard the others."

"So, you're the one who sent me the e-mail, too, Cary?"

"I thought that was Crash's e-mail I sent it to."

"No, it was mine." There's a pause, and I remember something else. "So, you also sent the super creepy note about stitches."

He grimaces. "I did. I guess I wanted to be sure whoever watched the video wouldn't go talking about it. I'm sorry."

I giggle. "I guess I can see that. But reading that alone in the bathroom stall at school was like being in the *Twilight Zone* or something."

He chuckles. "Why did you take it in the girl's bathroom?" His eyes go wide. "You know what, don't answer that." He looks at me expectantly.

"So now you want me to listen to this one."

He nods perceptively. "You've seen the others."

I roll my eyes. "This is true."

He holds up a handheld recording device. "Okay. Now you won't be able to see the video, but you can hear what they're saying anyway."

"I'm ready."

He hits play.

"What are you doing here? It's the middle of the day. You know I don't like the visibility." It's the creepy lady.

"I came to tell you I got the job."

"That's good I guess."

"It is good. Now I can monitor them up close. But there's so much chattering, I can't take them. They're always around, with their little heads together. They're plotting something I can tell."

The woman laughs. "Don't you remember being young? I bet they don't even see you. You're probably invisible, that's really what's bugging you. I bet you wish just one of them would notice."

"You've got it all wrong. I've perfected being invisible. I'm telling you, they know something. They're congregating every time I turn around. The quiet one, she's back in school. Maybe you were right about the body being staged. Surely she wouldn't be back so soon."

"If he's not dead, where is he? A loose end is never good. Find it." I shudder at her tone.

"I'm working on it. I gotta stay under the radar though."

"Cut through all the background bullshit. All you're hearing is the static. You've got to focus!"

"What do you mean?"

"Read between the lines. It's important. He could bury you." She's so evil, I've got goosebumps.

"Don't you think I know that? I'll find him. He's got to come up for air sometime."

"You think we've got all day? You've got to act now. Be quick about it. You've just got to know the questions so you can find the answers."

"What questions?" The guy sounds so clueless I *almost* feel sorry for him.

"Who would know where he is?"

"I can't go to the jail. I can't be seen there."

"There's got to be someone besides Tom who knows where he is."

"How do I find out?"

"Keep your eyes and ears open. Blend in. You should be able to do that. After all, aren't you The Neighbor?" There's heavy sarcasm in her voice.

"I hate adaptation. It's exhausting. I'm getting restless."

"Careful. Ecdysis is risky. And it's itchy." Weird. Now she's using scientific terms.

"What?"

"Never mind. Just blend. You can leave now." There's a few seconds of silence. "I told you to go. Why are you still here? An old lady needs her rest."

"Sleeping is all this place is good for. You're getting soft." His voice sounds threatening.

"Cold steel still rests beneath my pillow. Step a little closer if you think I'm bluffing." Her monotone voice gives no relief from her threatening words.

He coughs. "Relax. I just need to talk."

There's a mocking laugh. "You always want to talk. Should I get a couch and start charging you by the minute?"

"I'm telling you, something is up." His voice is nervous.

"Why do you say that?" She sounds exasperated.

"I was in the lunchroom and the girl grabbed the boy and they took off."

"So? They were probably just talking about a school project."

"I'm telling you. That girl is planning something. She knows."

"What does she know?"

"I don't know exactly, but she knows!" His anger and frustration come through the phone.

"What you're saying is crazy."

"I'm not crazy! Something's going down!"

"You're becoming a prisoner of your own fear. Get a grip."

"I'm not the prisoner. You're the one hiding out in this dark room all day. What are you running from this time?"

"Who says I'm hiding? I'm in here for my boy."

"Yeah, okay." There's an awkward pause.

"Listen closely, and you'll hear the music." Her words and tone send a chill down my spine.

"What music? What kind of medicine are they giving you?" Fear enters the man's voice.

"They're not giving me shit! The Pied Piper's playing. His volume's through the roof." The guy doesn't answer, so she keeps going. "It's time to put out the cheese. The rats are coming." I'm not sure I can listen to any more of her crazy talk.

"What cheese? What are you talking about?" He yells back at her.

There's more silence. "Go! Now! And watch out for the rats!" Her frantic whisper shout is scarier than anything I've heard her say yet.

Cary stops the player. I look over at Denver, who says nothing. I speak up. "She's gone completely nuthouse on us."

Denver shakes his head. "No, she hasn't. Everything that woman does is premeditated. She's probably just messing with The Neighbor."

I slap my dash. "Ugh. This is maddening. When are we going to find out his real name?"

Cary clears his throat. "Did you get anything from any of that?"

I sigh. "I don't know."

Denver looks over at my phone. "She's plotting. Something big's about to go down. If I were you, Cary, I'd stay close to Char and Crash."

———

I end the call and glance through my e-mails. "Ooh, an e-mail from Alex!"

Denver raises an eyebrow in question. "Who's Alex?" Do I detect jealousy? Surely not.

"The true crime writer!" I open the e-mail, pondering. "I don't know if I should tell him where she is. If I play my hand too early, it might blow everything, but if I don't tell him something, he might leave town."

"Tell him you're working on it, and you'll get back to him in a few days."

I swallow hard. "You really think this will take that long?"

"I have no idea."

It's another call from Cary. I pick up. "What is going on? You just called me like seconds ago."

Cary yells at me through the phone. "Your sister just called me up and chewed my butt good. She's so mad at you!"

I sigh. "Did you tell her what we're doing?"

"Yeah, I did. But she's convinced you're going to come home pregnant with Denver's kid." Denver chokes, and I try to turn the speaker off. "Do you have me on speaker?"

Denver answers before I can. "Yep."

"That's great. Denver, I swear if you lay a hand on Ciara."

I cough. "I'm a big girl, Cary. Please don't give me a talk about the birds and the bees."

He's not done yelling. "That's not funny! What are you two doing?"

"I told you before I left, Cary. We're going to crack this thing wide open. I can feel it." My excitement builds. What is wrong with me?

"Can't you feel it a little faster? Char's going to kill me before this is all through."

Denver winks at me. "Cary, stop taking orders from Char. You need to show her who's boss."

I punch Denver hard. "Don't listen to him, Cary. He's a misogynistic pig."

Denver puckers his lips at me and makes a kissing sound. "Ooh, big words. So sexy."

Cary's yelling again. "Stop flirting Mr. Sexy Pants, and focus." Char must've shared her favorite nickname for Denver with Cary. Great.

I can't take much more of this. "Is there a point to this phone call, Cary?"

"I don't want to be the messenger anymore, Ciara."

I feel bad that I'm making Cary talk to Char for me, but I just can't deal with one more thing right now. "It won't be much longer, Cary. I promise. Has anything happened since we last talked?"

"No."

Denver chimes in again. "Supposedly, there's a true crime writer in town looking for Ciara and me. He knew Tom's mother back in the day. He's trying to find her trail."

"Really?" Cary sounds doubtful, and I'm offended.

"Yes, Cary. I e-mailed him a while back. It was a hunch."

"A hunch? You contacted a stranger, a grown man, on a hunch?"

These guys are getting on my last nerve. "Cary. I know what I'm doing. It's called research. You should try it."

"Alright, alright, small Yengst. Don't get yourself all in a dither."

I smile and forgive him just a little. "Cary, you know I love that word."

"Yeah, yeah."

Denver calls out, "Find the writer. It shouldn't be hard. It's a small town."

Cary grunts. "Not as small as you think. Some people know how to hide things they don't want found."

Denver's jaw clenches at his words, and he doesn't answer. "Cary, please tell Char we're okay and we're being careful." I say and feel completely ridiculous. There's nothing safe about any of this, but it has to be done.

"Alright, Ciara. I guess I'll have to."

Denver sticks his tongue out at me. "We will be careful, but I can't promise there won't be any baby Evans coming!" He laughs out loud.

"Damn it, Den…!" I hang up the phone on Cary's furious hollering. "Denver! You're such a pig sometimes!" I punch him in the leg. He leans back, still laughing. "At least I thought it was funny."

———

We pop over a hill, and Denver turns off the highway. He drives down what looks like a deserted dirt road, but soon I see a few houses lining the streets. Most of them look abandoned, save for a few dogs wandering here and there. We drive a few blocks and then he takes a right, parking in front of an old stone garage. "This is it." I get out of the car. I walk beside him as he peers in the windows. He takes my hand and pulls me into an alleyway. We creep down the side of the building until we get toward the back end where I see a giant hole in the wall. He squats and sticks out his knee. "Let's go, Nancy."

I step high and put my foot on his thigh as I grab his shoulder. I hike one leg over and step into the building. His hand is on my butt, and he gives me a shove. Once I'm in, I turn around to glare at him. "Did you really need to grab my butt?"

He throws his hands up. "I was just trying to be helpful. Give me a hand up while I climb the wall." I manage to help tug him up the side of the building. The garage is big and dark. It takes a few minutes for my eyes to acclimate. We wander along the side of the wall. He breathes a little faster. "That's it. I can't believe it's here."

I follow him to an old, brown, nondescript car. He opens the car door. It squeaks noisily. I swallow hard as I see the bullet holes in the door. He crawls in the backseat, feeling around before he lays down. "Do you know how many nights I slept in this seat? More than I can count." I say nothing, as I don't think he's waiting for an answer. "My mom and I spent a summer with my aunt. I guess that's all the longer they could stand each other."

I look back at him. "What happened?"

He laughs bitterly. "Oh, at first it was kind of fun. We spent a lot of time at the beach, and I played with Tom. But then after a few days of that, things changed and we started living in the car, I think. I just know I spent a lot of nights on this seat by myself. I remember being scared they wouldn't come back every time they left me."

My heart breaks for the scared little boy he must have been. "I'm sorry, Denver. I had no idea."

He shrugs. "That's in the past. I made it through. I'm still here." I study him a few seconds and bite my tongue. I'm not so sure he's okay. I turn away to search the console and then the glovebox. I remove everything carefully. I'm slightly annoyed to find a car maintenance diary, which I toss at him. I keep searching.

I hear the pages turn as he thumbs through it. "Ciara."

I turn back to look at him. He's dropped the book beside him on the seat. "I know, it's nothing."

He shakes his head at me. "It's not nothing. It's her kill record."

I shiver at his words. "Excuse me?"

"It's a list of everyone she's killed."

I look back at the book on the seat and shudder at the thought. "Are you sure? Are there names in there?"

He shakes his head back and forth. "There are initials and dates though."

"Why would she write them down?"

His eyes look dead. "I don't know, but she did."

I can hardly look at him. "Is your mom's... you know, is she in there?"

He glances down the list, sighing. "No."

A small excitement grows. "Do you think your mom is still...alive?"

"No. If she were, she would have come for me. I know it." I study him. His jawline's as hard as granite, and his lips should be outlawed, but when I look in his eyes, I see a lost little boy.

I drop my gaze as I try to think. "But if her name isn't on there..."

He tosses the book against the door. "Maybe she had someone else do it." I hate the defeat in his voice.

"So, we have the book, now what?"

His hand clobbers the top of my head. He shoves me down into the front seat. "Get down!" He whispers. I duck, and he hits the floor behind my seat.

"Someone's in here." It's the woman! How did they find us so fast?

"Do you really think they're here?" I fight panic as I hear the man's voice I've come to recognize so well. I really hate The Neighbor.

"That's her car outside. I can't believe he figured it out so quickly. I've got to get that book before they do." The footsteps get closer and closer. I have no idea what I'm going to do. I hear Denver cock the gun. I pray I don't die. The footsteps stop. "Did you hear something?" There's another pause. "Oh, nep-hew." I thought I'd heard the creepiest tone I could hear until now. The woman's sing-song voice is ten times worse than her creepy laughter.

"Maybe they're not here." The man sounds nervous.

"Grow a pair. They're here. I can feel it in my bones." The footsteps start again. The sound of gunfire fills the air, and I roll off the front seat to hit the floor. I duck my head beneath the dash.

"What the hell you doin' in my shed?" a deep voice barks.

"Relax, old man. We were just antiquing." The man barks out the answer.

"This here's private property, and you're trespassing. I'm within my rights to shoot you."

A throat clears. "Easy, now. We're coming out. We are unarmed." The man's voice is slow and even. "Our hands are in the air."

"They're here. I can feel it," she whispers to him.

A gun cocks. "Hurry it up. I ain't got all day."

"Sir, I think you have a car in here that belongs to my family. If I could just take a look." Her voice sounds almost natural.

"Lady, this is my garage. All that shit belongs to me. You don't go pokin' around in other people's junk without permission unless you aim to get shot."

Denver whispers to me. "Amen to that."

I'm too scared to answer.

"Did you hear that? I think there's someone in your garage." She's not ready to give up.

"I didn't hear a dang thing except the two of you. Now get out of here before I call the cops."

"I'll make it worth your time. All I want is just a peek." My cheeks blush at her suggestive tone.

Another shot fires and I flinch again. "I told you, lady. Get out of here and don't come back."

"We hear you, sir, we're leaving." The man's talking again. A few minutes pass by and then a car starts. I breathe easy as the engine sounds get quieter and quieter.

Minutes go by and we lay here, not moving an inch. Just about the time I start to relax, a man's head pops in the window, and I about jump out of my skin. Denver pops up from the backseat with his gun pointing at the man, who smiles down at us. "Is that any way to greet an old friend?"

I glance at Denver, whose gun hasn't moved. "Who are you?" he growls at the old man.

The man keeps his gaze on Denver. "I'm an old friend of your mom's. I knew this day would come. I mean, I kind of didn't want it to, but..." He gets no response. "Are you going to lower that gun, son?"

"I'm not your son." The air grows heavy in the car.

The man chuckles. "No, you're not. I'm your uncle. My name's Cy."

I study the man. I notice his gun hasn't moved from his side. I reach over and touch the top of Denver's gun to push it downward. He slowly lowers his gun. "You're my uncle?"

He nods his head. "Yep."

Denver sits back in the seat. "I didn't know I had an uncle." The man opens the door and climbs in the backseat to sit by Denver. "Your mom always was tight-lipped. It seemed like she only told me what she needed me to know, and apparently that wasn't much." Denver doesn't answer. The man turns to me. "I don't know about you two, but all this running around made me hungry. Why don't you come inside? I make a pretty mean pot of chili." He looks back at Denver. "And bring that blasted book with you. I'm about ready to burn it."

That gets Denver's attention, as he snatches it up, shoves it up under his shirt, and holds it in place as we crawl out of the car.

18

We cross the street and follow him into his house. I cringe as Denver hasn't let go of his gun. My insides jump as the old man opens his front door, and I hear a howling. Two fat and happy short-legged dogs come trotting out. Their ears drag on the ground as they raise their heads in greeting, howling once more. "Rambo and Sly, quit your howling." They hush up and rub up against his legs.

I lean down to scratch their ears. He spins around on us. "You'd better come eat some grub. I imagine those two will be back by dark. We'd best be ready."

My stomach turns hard as a rock. What have I gotten myself into, and how can I escape? "I don't think that's necessary. We found what we were looking for. Denver, you ready to go?"

"No, he's right. It ends here. Tonight." Denver's unwavering tone cuts through me. His words of acceptance are so final.

There's got to be another way. "Denver, what does that mean? Now that we have the list, can't we call the cops?"

The man looks at me and then Denver. "No cops. We've got to beat her at her own game."

I step backwards from the kitchen into the living room, feeling like I've just fallen into a deep pit. "Count me out. I'm having no part of whatever this is." I stare at Denver. I feel so betrayed. "You knew he was here this whole time. I'm such an idiot." I pace back and forth, trying to keep my calm, but it's not working. I need some space.

I go to leave the room, but the old man grabs me. The strength in his grip surprises me as he tugs me to the kitchen table. "You're not going anywhere. Just sit down and listen, cause I'm only saying this once." I sit down in the chair that he helps me into. I cram my hands between my knees to hide my trembling fingers. "There's a tunnel that leads out of this house. It runs clear out to the back shed. The trapdoor out there is covered with a heavy chair, so you'll have to push kind of hard, but it *will* open."

I stare wide-eyed at the old man. I feel like I'm in the middle of the Cuban missile crisis. "Are you like a Doomsday kind of guy?"

He laughs at me. "That would make more sense than the trouble we're in. Ever since my brother fell for his mother," he points at Denver, "I've had nothing but trouble at my backdoor." He looks back at me. "Survival's a way of life I've had to learn."

Denver looks back at him. "My mom was innocent. It's her crazy sister who's the killer."

I study the old man. "She's got something on you too, doesn't she? That's why you don't want any cops involved."

He shakes his finger in my face. "That damn woman laid a trap, and I walked right into it. I made *one* mistake, and she's held it over my head ever since. She's the reason I can't go to the cops. But this ends tonight! I'll burn this place to the ground if I have to, just so long as she's in it!"

I flinch at his words. "You're giving up your house?"

The old man slams his fist down on the table, making me jump. "That damn woman ruined my life! She's the reason I've never had a family of my own! I was too afraid and too stupid to call her bluff. I'm sixty-eight years old and I'm tired of living in fear! I want to wake up in the morning and breathe freely. And after today I'll be free here or on the other side, but it ends here."

His words fly around the room, strangling me. I don't know how to answer him.

Denver sits down. He looks up at the old red-faced old man, whose chest heaves. "Okay, I'm in."

I search the room, praying for a viable excuse to put a stop to this miniature Armageddon. I spy his dogs. "What about them?"

He smiles at me. "I wasn't sure before, but now I know. Since you're here, you're going to take them down the tunnel and wait. Me and Denver will do the dirty work. You don't have to take part in any of it."

I shake my head and look over at Denver. My heart sinks. "I know your plan. I'm already a part of it."

Denver looks up at his uncle. "How are the two of us going to overpower the two of them?"

The man smiles and looks past Denver. I almost fall over as Denver's another man walks in the room. "Hey, son."

His voice is different, his eyes are bright and clear. His walk is swift and purposeful. He looks years younger than the old man I saw in the shadowy shed.

"Dad?" Denver whispers. I'm stunned.

He sneaks by the stove and spoons up some chili in a bowl before plopping it down in front of Denver. "Eat up."

The practiced familiarity is too much. Denver's eyes fill with tears as he stares into the bowl. "I don't understand."

His dad sighs as he sits down across from him. "I've done everything I can to keep you safe, Denver, and I hope when this is all over, you remember that."

Denver shoves his bowl away. "So this whole time you've been pretending?"

"I had to. It was all to keep you safe. I thought if she didn't see me as a threat, she would leave you alone."

"You acted like a crazy, senile old man just to keep me safe? I could have had a normal life. I could have played sports. I could have had a place to come home to after school instead of sleeping in cars and on people's couches!" Denver looks away, shaking his head. "This is so messed up."

"I'm sorry, son. You don't know who you're foolin' with. She took your mother away from me, and I was afraid she'd take you next."

Denver looks up at his dad with tears rolling down his cheeks. "Why? Why would she do that to her own sister?"

His dad looks back at him. "Because she can."

I can't stand the suspense any longer. "Who is this woman?"

His dad looks up at me. "When she was seven years old, her parents died in Desert Storm, leaving her and her sister, who was six at the time, behind. They went to live with their grandma, who was a very frugal woman. The grandma put all their money away in savings from their parents dying in an account for their college tuition, but Stella was always greedy. She wanted more than her grandma would give her. As soon as she was old enough, she married a small-town boy and left her grandma's house as fast as she could.

"As soon as Stella got pregnant with Tom, she went out and found trouble. She dragged her husband into it, and he got shot. Stella then shot the man who shot her husband. She went back to her grandma's house and demanded her inheritance. When the grandma wouldn't give it to her, Stella burned her house down with her grandma in it and collected the life insurance. Luckily, her little sister was at a friend's house. When her little sister caught up to her, Stella threatened her and told her if she didn't do exactly what she said, she would be next."

I sit down. "What a psychopath."

The uncle knocks on the countertop. "Yep. And now that psychopath's after you. So, you'd better let us help you. Don't even think about takin' off, 'cause she'll track you down."

I shake my head. "I can't believe all of this is over $3,000.00. That's all my brother owed the guy."

The uncle looks back at me. "It's not just about the money with Stella. It's a game, and she'll stop at nothing to win."

Denver's dad taps the table with his knuckles. "Yeah, but if she thinks you owe her something, she won't let up until she gets it."

19

Denver taps the table. "So, how are we going to set this house on fire?"

The brothers sit at the table. I see a little of both of them in Denver as I watch their hands. His dad answers. "First, we need some bait."

Denver takes his pack and dumps the money on the table in front of his dad. "There's your bait."

His dad grins at him. "I was hoping that was you who found it, and not somebody else."

Denver grins up at me. "Ciara's the one who figured it out. She's quite the detective." He gives me a wink, and I blush at his words of praise.

I sit down at the head of the table and look out at the three of them. "How do we contact her? Does anyone have her phone number?" No one says anything. "Great."

Denver's dad answers again. "I'm tellin' you that doesn't matter, because she loves the game too much to not come back."

His brother pipes up. "And when she does, we'll be ready."

I look over at Denver. "Can I talk to you?"

He eyes the money on the table. He leaves it there as he gets up, but he keeps the gun in his pants. "Sure."

I don't know where I'm going, only that it has to be far enough they can't hear me. He must sense my confusion as he takes my hand. "Let's walk the tunnel you're going to be in tonight." I follow him through the kitchen into the laundry room.

I take my phone in my pocket and check to be sure I have plenty of battery. I step back as he opens the door up sideways off the floor. I follow him down the narrow set of stairs, feeling weird as the door slowly closes above him. I turn my phone flashlight on and check the ground for any rats, but all I see is a lot of soft dirt, as I smell the earth. It's all quiet and cool. I feel completely alone with Denver once more. My heart trips over itself at the thought.

"This might be the last time we're together." I look over at Denver, hating that I sound all dramatic. I get no warning before he bumps me up against the wall. His mouth comes crashing down on mine. For one crazy hot moment, I think he's forgotten everyone else too. Every part of me burns everywhere, and I don't want it to stop until his hand goes too far, and I freeze. "Denver, I'm sorry, but I can't."

He looks at me. "Isn't that what you want?"

Yes. "No. I wanted some time with you alone to talk." And to make out if I'm being honest with myself.

"Oh."

I kick the side of the wall with the back of my foot as I lean on it. "I mean, that was very nice too, but..."

"Nice? You think making out with me is nice?"

I'm not used to these conversations. "I thought it was crazy hot, okay? I just... I just don't want to talk about it. Gabi talks about it, like all the time, and it's so annoying."

He steps up to me again. His hand grips my hip as he leans down. "I'm not your girlfriend, Ciara. I'm the guy kissing you, and I like to know what drives you crazy." His words fill my ears, and I'm not sure how to answer. He sighs and moves away from me. I want to reach out and grab his shirt to pull him back. "I'm dying over here, Ciara. I want you. So bad."

What? Did I just hear what I thought I heard? From Denver? "You want me?"

"Yes. You. Not Gabi, or any other girl. Just you." I stare at him. I want so much to believe what he's saying.

"Why?"

He snorts. "I can't believe you just asked me that. You're solid." I blush. I hate that he used that word. "Solid as in nothing breaks you. You're unshakable. You know how many girls would have bailed on me by now?"

I look away. "Ones that are smarter than me."

"No, Ciara. Bailed because they were afraid, because they couldn't handle it. But not you. Nothing scares you."

I stare at him leaning on the wall. An awkward silence starts. It grows bigger and bigger as he looks down at the ground. I sneak peeks at him, still leaning on the wall. I take a deep breath, knowing I'll have to make the next move, another thing I've never done before. I walk over to stand in front of him. "Denver." I whisper his name.

His head comes up. His eyes burn into mine. "Yeah."

I step closer and reach out to put my hands on his hips. "You scare me."

He leans in and hovers above my lips. "Why?"

"Because if I fall..." I don't finish my sentence because I've got a mouth full of Denver.

His kiss goes on and on, and he doesn't let up. His hands roam freely, but so do mine.

Minutes feel like hours before he finally raises his head as he pulls me to him, and I rest my cheek on his chest. "I've already fallen."

I hug him tighter, feeling like I'm in a dream. I can't believe Denver Evans has fallen for me. I stand here, enjoying the quiet, but my doubts won't stay away. "Denver, you don't have to do this. There's an exit at the end, like he said. We could leave now. We could get away."

He holds me tighter. "Yes, Ciara I do. I'm doing it for my mom and I'm doing it for me."

I step away, feeling cold. "No, you don't. We could just leave. Right now. Your dad and uncle could handle those two. We didn't ask for this."

He crosses his arms on his chest. "You can leave, Ciara. You can make your escape, but this is *my* family, and I'm not leaving until she's dealt with. The woman has hurt too many people, and it has to stop."

"Denver! You're eighteen years old! You've got your whole life in front of you!"

"I'm seventeen, Ciara. I won't be eighteen until next week. That's why this has to end tonight."

I blink my eyes in disbelief. "You're going to take the fall, aren't you? For whatever happens here tonight. You'll take the fall because they won't try you as an adult."

He kicks the dirt. "You were always too smart for your own good, Ciara."

I try again. "You don't owe them anything, Denver. You said so yourself, they've never been there for you."

"Ciara, you don't understand. They're my family. They did everything they could to keep me safe until now. That woman has taken everything from me! And I'm done letting her push me around."

My head reels and I start to pace. "What are we doing here, Denver?"

He grabs my hand and grips it tight. "We're walking all the way down this tunnel, so you know where you're going tonight to make your escape." I walk fast as he drags me along. I try to wiggle out of his grip, but he won't let me.

Nothing matters anymore, and I can't keep it all in as I stumble unwillingly down the tunnel, led by Denver, the force of nature. "It figures the one boy I would fall in love with is a criminal."

He backs me against the wall again and gets in my face. Oh, deliciousness. "I'm not a criminal."

"Yes, you are. You broke into the school, you stole your dad's money, and now you're planning to burn down a house with someone in it." Why can't I keep my mouth shut?

He bumps his hips against mine. "If I'm a criminal, Ciara, so are you. You did all of those things with me."

I start to protest. "That's different. I was trying to help you, and my brother."

His hands trace circles on the small of my back. "And how is that different from what I'm doing?"

I press my palms on the wall, trying to cool down. "It's different because you're out for revenge!"

His hands grip my hips again. "Damn right I want revenge! I'm tired of being taken, Ciara. I'm going to take what I want for a change." If I thought his kisses couldn't get any hotter, I was so wrong. Before I know it, my hands are around his neck, and my hand is in his hair. I'm plastered against Denver. I stand on tippy toe. As quickly as his assault started, it stops. He backs away and his hands are all trembly. He clears his throat. "Let's go find that trap door before I take you to the floor."

My ears burn, and I step away, putting more distance between us.

―――――

We finally get to the end, and he starts pushing around on the ceiling. I hear something up above! I grab his arm and yank him down to squat beside me. "Ciara, what?"

I clamp my hand over his mouth and lean in to whisper in his ear. "Someone's up there. I heard them."

"I'm telling you there's nothing here." It's The Neighbor.

"Something is. I just can't put my finger on it." The creepy old woman answers.

"This is a waste of time, Stella. I'm out of here."

A gunshot fires. There's a heavy thud right above us. I drop to my knees and crawl toward the wall, away from the blood that drips from the ceiling. "You're a waste of time, Stanley. I have no use for you."

I look up. Denver tears through the tunnel. I start out after him. I'm terrified when I hear a door swing open from up above. There are footsteps! Gunshots bounce off the walls.

I call out to him. "Wait, Denver! Wait for me!"

I run faster. I have to get away from the footsteps in the dark behind me. I almost trip as I zigzag blindly in the dark, as more bullets ricochet off the walls. I'm almost to the end when I trip over a foot! Denver lays on the ground. I take his gun and fire back to buy us some time. I grab his other arm. "Come on, Denver. Get up!"

"I can't walk."

My heart races. I yank as hard as I can on his arm. "Don't let her win, Denver. Get up!"

He stumbles off the ground. He limps heavily as we make it up the cellar steps and shove the door open. I push him up and out and scramble out behind him. I'm terrified to see her face peek around the wall before I slam the heavy door into the floor. "Get something heavy and put it against this door!" I yell.

More shots fire! I jump clear away from the door and sit on the edge, holding it down with my feet. Denver lays against the wall, moaning. No one comes. Why is the house empty? Where is everyone? "Help!" I call out. The deafening shots stop, but she pushes against the door. I look over at Denver, and he's passed out cold. I don't know what to do. She shoves the door open. Her hand is on the edge. I stomp on it as hard as I can. Her gun hand comes around. I don't think. I just react. I kick her gun hand as hard as I can before I kick her square in the face.

She cries out, drops her weapon and the door. It comes down on her other hand, still holding on to the ledge. I jump up and down on the door like a maniac as I stare down at her fingers. I will them to disappear and try desperately to ignore her howling. All I can think of is

Denver needs help. I manage to focus through my rage and hysteria to see her fingers are no longer sticking out. I stop jumping long enough to reach for my phone. It's gone! "Crap!" I must have dropped it in the tunnel. I lean over and yank Denver's from his back pocket and call 911.

"911, what is your location?"

I can't think at all. "Hell!"

"Ma'am, I would advise you not to prank this phone line. What is your location?"

"Doesn't your GPS tell you? I have no idea! I have a gunshot victim." My throat closes at my words. I start to cry. "Please get here. Hurry!"

Denver's uncle and dad show up. "What is going on?"

I point at the door. "She found the tunnel! She followed us, and she shot Denver."

More shots hit the door, and I duck. I scramble against the wall, dropping the phone. I hold my ears. The uncle looks over at me. "How many rounds does she have?"

"I don't know! This is the third time she's fired on us this time."

I wait for the door to open now that the firing stopped, but it doesn't. I look at them and they look at me as if to say, now what?

I swallow hard. "I called 911."

His dad looks down at Denver lying on the floor. "What? Why?"

"He's been shot!"

The uncle rolls him over. "Where's the blood?"

Denver opens his eyes and reaches for his ankle, still groaning. "I didn't get shot."

His dad stares down at him. "Why were you laying on the floor then?"

He looks up at his dad. "I rolled my bad ankle. It might be broken."

"Oh."

"It's throbbing."

"What do we do about Stella?" I ask.

The uncle cracks open the cellar door. We all get back, expecting a gun, but there's just empty darkness. "Stella! We have your money!" he roars into the darkness.

We get no response. I think I hear heavy breathing, but I'm so worked up it might be my own.

Denver's phone is still in my hand, and I dial 911 again.

"911, can I help you?"

I almost laugh out loud. "We don't need an ambulance. There's been a misunderstanding. There is no gunshot wound."

"Ma'am, we can't just cancel the ambulance."

A phone rings in the background and I hear another dispatcher say, "Colleen, there's a major car wreck. They're needing all the ambulances they can get." There's silence on the other end. I hang up the phone.

Denver's dad leaves the room and returns with a big flashlight. "I'm going down there."

Denver pulls his gun from his jeans. "Take this with you."

His dad grins and pulls up his shirt. "That's alright. I've got my Glock." His brother follows right behind.

Denver butt scoots himself into the living room. I go to the kitchen to make an ice bag. I wrap it with a towel. He sits on the floor and leans against the couch. "Lay on your back and put your foot up on the couch. It'll help with the swelling."

He maneuvers himself around and sticks his foot up until his ankle rests on the couch cushion. I sit down beside him and hold the ice on his ankle. He stares up at the ceiling. "Have you got any Vicodin?"

I giggle. "Nope. Those are in my other purse."

Denver looks up at me. "Ciara."

He sounds so serious. "Yeah."

"Thanks for taking care of me."

I lean back on the couch, unsure of how to answer, as I squeeze his other foot. "Does that mean you're done being stupid?"

He frowns up at me. "What does that mean?"

I wave toward the cellar door. "The woman! Are you done messing with her? She shot a guy! Right above our heads!"

He looks away. "It ain't over 'til it's over."

I swat his foot. "Don't you start talking in idioms like your cousin, Tom."

He glares back at me. "I was this close, Ciara. We almost got her."

A throat clears, and his dad steps into the room. "I'd say you got her. There's a pretty good trail of blood going down that tunnel. She won't go far."

Denver looks back at me. "At least we can all sleep well tonight, knowing she won't be back."

The uncle laughs. "As long as that bitch is alive and breathing and money's on the table, I'd sleep with one eye open if I was you."

I look around. "Where are the dogs?"

He frowns. "I took them next door to the neighbors. They're stayin' there overnight. I didn't want them getting' hurt."

Denver looks backwards at his uncle from his spot on the floor. "What'd you tell your neighbor?"

He shrugs. "I told her to keep her doors locked because things might get a little hairy tonight."

I snort. "And she accepted that answer?"

He eyeballs me. "Yeah. We live in ghost towns 'cause we don't want people in our business. She appreciated my warning."

I stop asking questions. He leaves the room, and Denver's hand slides up my calf, giving me all the feels. I twitch. "What are you doing?"

He looks up at me, all heavy-lidded. "Are you going to sleep with me tonight?"

"Excuse me?"

"Down here. Are you going to stay down here tonight with me?"

Heck, yes. Thinking about being anywhere in this house without him creeps me right out. I shrug my shoulders. "I suppose." I glance down at him again, trying to sound stern. "But you gotta behave."

A wolfish grin fills his face, and my face flames. "I behaved on your couch."

That was a long time ago, before I told him I loved him and before he told me I drive him crazy.

I nudge his sore ankle, feeling mean as he winces. "How's your ankle?"

He grins through his pain as he looks back at me, tracing the back of my calf. "You think causing me a little pain's going to distract me from what I'm after?"

Someone stomps on the floor, and we both look up to see his dad staring at the two of us. I feel like an idiot. "Denver."

His hand drops and he cranes his neck to look backwards at his dad. "Yeah?"

"Lay off."

I cross my arms beneath my chest and look around the room. His dad turns to me with a smile as he holds my phone up. "Found this on the stairs. I thought you might want it." He slaps it in my palm.

"Thanks."

20

I feel Denver's eyes on me as mine roam around the room. "Checking the place for weapons?"

I giggle. "Maybe." I sit here a few minutes. I pull out my phone. I feel bad as I see text after text from Char. I text her back. "I'm safe."

I see a text from Ari, and my eyes water, as I realize she's the only friend I've got who's texted me in two days. "I'm still with Denver. We are safe. Should be home soon."

I look down at Denver and recall the day we met. "You got any cards?"

He laughs out loud. "Yes!"

Denver and I play cards 'til midnight when I finally give in and let him up on the couch. He lays down, props his foot up at the end, and I snuggle up against him, feeling all cozy and warm. Minutes later, we're fast asleep.

I wake to the sound of someone in the kitchen. The hairs on the back of my neck stick straight up, and I start to shake Denver to wake him, but then I think better of the idea. I lean down and kiss his lips. Just as I suspected, he's wide awake. I pull myself away, clamp my hand over his mouth to shush him, and point to the kitchen. His eyes get really big.

We barely get off the couch, and I smell smoke! I race to the kitchen. I spy her with her back to me. For a few seconds, I'm as mesmerized as she appears to be as she stares up at the kitchen curtains going up in flames, but then I spy the cash lying on the table, and it pisses me off to think she's going to walk out with it.

I run at the table, shove the money hard to the far end, and watch it fall to the floor. She turns around slowly, and that's when I see her whole side is covered in blood. Her face is white as a sheet. She's sweating profusely, but still, she manages an answer. *"That's my money!"* Her voice comes out in a roar, and I know I've just pushed a psychopath over the edge.

I don't think as I react. I pick up a chair and chuck it at her. She puts her hands up to block it, but she's too weak. It hits her and she falls to the floor. I run to the other end of the table and grab the piles of cash.

She lies on the floor, shaking; as a puddle of blood starts to form. Her eyes stay glued to the cash in my hand. I hold the money high and wave it around wildly. "You want your money? Here!" I touch it to the flaming curtains and watch her eyes go wide.

She reaches out to me. "No! That's my money! I killed for that money."

I drop it in the sink and hold another brick, and then another, lighting them all on fire in front of her. I go for the last one. "Ciara!" I stop when I hear Denver's voice. "Stop! We need one for evidence."

I lay it down on the table, breathing hard as I stand a few feet away from her. She moves slightly, and I see the gun, but it's too late. She stretches out her hand and pulls the trigger. There's a loud shot, and Denver goes crashing down on top of her! "No!"

I hear nothing. I see nothing. My shoulder's on fire.

The next thing I know, I'm looking into the face of a police officer. I say the first thing that comes to mind. "Where's Denver?"

The cop shakes his head. "You're not going to Colorado, sweetheart. You're in Kansas." I try to grab his arm to make him understand, but a burning pain shoots through my arm. "Careful, sweetheart. You've been shot."

I growl at him. "Stop calling me sweetheart. Where's everybody at?"

"The woman went to the morgue."

I close my eyes, relieved. "Oh, thank God."

"Ciara!" I must be dreaming. How did Char find me? "Ciara!" She shoves him out of the way.

I giggle. "Char, you just assaulted a police officer."

She holds me close. "He's an EMT." She wheels around on him. "Which hospital are you going to? I'm a nurse."

He looks back at her. "Are you related?"

I take Char's hand. "She's my sister."

He turns back to her. "The hospital's about thirty miles from here. It looks like a clean shot. There shouldn't be any complications. Her vitals were all within normal limits. She should be stable for transfer."

She looks back at him. "Thank you, sir. I do apologize for bumping into you."

He grabs a hold of the stretcher I'm lying on before glaring back at her. "Is that what we're calling it? I'll see you at the hospital."

They roll me out the front door. I grab at Char's arm. "Where's Denver?"

She glances down at me. "Ciara, forget about that boy. Let's just get you taken care of."

21

The first couple of nights home are the worst. I sleep in Char's room with her, and she finally takes a few days off. Things slowly improve, except for waking up in the night in a cold sweat from another nightmare, wishing Denver was beside me.

A few weeks later, I return to school. I'm *kind of* a celebrity. Gabi still hasn't forgiven me for taking off with Denver, but as I've learned through all of this, there are worse things to worry about than her wrath. I miss Denver, and I still look for him in the empty spaces. Our couch, my room, my car, the breakfast table, and pretty much everywhere else. It surprises me how one person could fill up so much of my life so quickly.

In the meantime, I've been taking it easy, spending more time with Char and Crash. That's one good thing that's happened since I got shot. We're all closer than we were before.

At school, Ari and Esmee have stuck by my side through all the ugly rumors, and that's been awesome.

I've gotten a few e-mails from Alex Smith, but I've ignored them. I don't have much to say. Denver's gone, and I don't feel it's my right. Stella was Denver's aunt, and that's his family business. School's out, and I'm walking down a quiet hallway, when an arm reaches out from behind a door and grabs my hand! Sparks fly up my arm. It's Denver. I'd know his smell anywhere. I hold up my phone to light up his face as he shuts the door and smiles down at me.

I throw an arm around his neck, as I raise up on tippy toes to kiss him. "Where have you been?"

He gives me a small smile. "Here and there."

"Are you coming back to school, then?"

He shakes his head back and forth. "Nah. I think I'll just get my GED."

I can't believe this. "You're dropping out?"

His jaw clenches. "I'm getting my GED. I can't stay here."

I touch his face. "You could stay with us again. Stella's gone now. There's no threat."

He backs up. "I can't stay here, Ciara."

"Then what are you doing here?"

He takes my hand. "Will you take a drive with me?"

Yes. Anywhere. "Alright."

He looks at me again. "Will you turn off your tracker?"

"What? No, I can't do that. Char will be all over my butt in two seconds."

I open the door, and he follows me out, still holding my hand. I go red as I spy Ari down the hall. She laughs, shaking her head. "What is it with you two and closets?"

I get closer. "It's not what you think, Ari."

She giggles. "I know that. I know you, Ciara."

I hold out my phone. "Could you hold on to this for a while? I'm taking a ride, and Char will have my butt if I leave town."

Ari stares Denver down. "Where are you going?"

He gives her his signature swoon-worthy grin. "It's a surprise."

Ari doesn't smile back. "You bring her back tonight. In one piece. We all know what happened last time the two of you went off together."

Denver frowns at her. "That was..." Ari raises her eyebrows at him and puts her hands on her hips. "That's really not fair."

Ari waves her finger in his face and grabs my elbow. "Denver, life ain't fair. I call 'em like I see 'em. You take good care of my friend." Ari side hugs me. "I mean it, Ciara. Don't make me sorry I'm covering for you."

I exit the school walking on air. I float past a gawking Gabi who stops mid-sentence to watch Denver walk by. She steps away from her group and walks up to Denver. "Hi, Denver." I can't believe she's stroking his arm right in front of me.

He shakes her off. "Gabi, I've got two things to say to you." She looks up at him from beneath her long dark curly lashes, smiling her little smile. "Ciara is *not* a slut. Stop spreading ugly rumors about her."

Denver's voice is so loud, he's almost yelling. There's no way her group didn't hear him. I'm so shocked, all I can do I is stare at the ground. He nudges me. "Chin up."

Gabi's eyes narrow as she looks at me. I say nothing as the smile disappears from her face. She sticks out her lip and pouts before she turns and flounces back to her group.

We continue walking until we get to my car. I hop in, ready for more time with Denver, who's still staring at me. I turn to him. "What?"

"Would you like to get a piece of pie with me at the café in the next town over?"

"Sure." I have no idea where this is going, but I know I have to make a stop as we pass by my house. I run upstairs, grab something, and stuff it in a sack. I giggle all the way down the stairs, thinking about Denver's face when I give it to him.

The car ride is quiet as we drive down the highway. We walk into the café and take a seat. A guy at the bar turns to look at us. Denver waves him over, and he sits down across from us. "Hi, I'm Alex Smith."

My hands fly under the table in my nervousness. Denver takes a hold of my hand, and I find my voice. "I'm Ciara Yengst."

He grins. "I know. Since we last e-mailed, I've been speaking with Denver at length, and I've decided to write a book about his aunt, Stella Edwards."

I turn to Denver. "Are you okay with this?"

He looks back at me. "Only if you are."

I'm confused. "But it's your family, Denver."

He nods. "Kind of. She's my aunt. But the story is kind of centered around you."

"Me?" My face flames red. "Why me?"

Alex smiles at me. "Denver tells me you're quite the detective. He says you have a real knack for it."

I feel exposed. "I don't know about that. I mean, I was just trying to keep my brother out of trouble. That's all."

He taps his pen on the table. "That may be so, but you managed to bust a major drug dealer and catch a serial killer."

I shudder at the thought, embarrassed to be asking my next question. "She's dead, right? She's gone?"

Denver shifts uncomfortably in his seat. "Yeah, Ciara. She's gone for good."

Alex shoves some papers in front of me. "These are consent forms giving me permission to write about you."

I skim over them, feeling weird. "I would feel better if my sister looked these over."

He chuckles. "Denver told me you were smart."

I look back at him. "I'd also like to send you e-mails. I would feel better if I typed up my experiences."

He nods his head. "Sounds good to me. Just send me PDF files, double-spaced, Times Roman, size 12 font."

I reach out my hand to shake his. "You've got it." I clear my throat. "Do you think you'd have time to stop by my house if Char allows it?"

He gives me a wink. "Just let me know when and where. I'll be around for a few more days." He crawls out of the booth and walks away.

Denver turns to me with a confused look on his face. "Ciara, that was Alex Smith. I thought you'd be more excited."

I lean on his shoulder and enjoy the feel of him. "It was nice to see him, Denver. But I just want to see you."

He turns to face me. "I want to see you, too."

The waitress stops at our table. She blushes as she looks down at Denver. "Are y'all ready to order?"

I scan the menu and inspiration hits me. "I think I'd like a brownie and some lemonade."

Denver shakes his head and shuts my menu. "Scratch that. We'd like two pieces of apple pie and a couple of ice teas." I'm furious at him for ordering for me, but I say nothing, as I still can't believe he's here. He hands the menus back to the waitress. He turns back to me. "Ciara, I'm sorry I took over your order, but brownies are for saying hello. Pies are for saying goodbye."

My lip trembles, and I bite down hard. I turn away to hide my tears. "Why did you come back if you're just going to leave me again?"

"I wanted to see you one more time. I needed to be sure you're okay."

I slap the table. "I *was* okay, Denver. I was *fine* until you showed up."

He looks back at me and takes my hand. "Ciara, you're the only person who's ever been completely honest with me. Are you sorry you met me?"

I laugh because I can't help it. "Let's see. Since I met you, I've been shot at, done a B&E, lost half of my social media followers, ruined my reputation, and now I'm serving community service."

His eyes get wide. "Community service?"

I roll my eyes. "Yeah, Char is making me and Crash work at the nursing home for free until she decides we've learned our lesson about making stupid mistakes."

He chuckles. "Man, your sister really is a warden."

I giggle. "Yep. You don't mess with nurses."

His thumb nail grazes my skin. "Ciara, are you okay?"

I take a deep breath. "You broke my heart, Denver. You're the first boy who's ever looked at me like a boy looks at a girl." I turn to stare out the window. I feel embarrassed, but I'm also angry. I whip back around and look him in the eye. "I've got something to say, and you need to hear it."

I stare at him and see the lost boy I met so long ago, but his soft edges are gone, and there's a hardness in his eyes that wasn't there before. I give it one last shot. "I love you. So much. But none of that matters if you don't love yourself."

He looks away first. "I'm working on that."

I study him and wonder where he's heading. "You're going to walk the straight and narrow now, right? No more criminal activity?"

He locks his fingers between mine, leans over, and talks low in my ear. "You know a lot of criminals are also geniuses."

I can't help it. I giggle a little before turning back to face him. "You're done with all the mischief, though, right? I mean, you're not really going to continue down that road." I shift in my seat and hate that I feel like I'm lecturing him, but I do my best to make him see reason. "It'll only get worse, you know. Next time you might not be so lucky."

He frowns at me. "Ciara, I hear you. Loud and clear. I'm not chasing any more trouble, but I can't stay here. Not even for you, but I wanted to leave you a souvenir of us, and that's why I contacted Alex."

My mind flies to our heated make-out sessions. What? "I'm not putting the story of us in that book. No way."

He laughs. "Maybe you could put like a kid-friendly version of a beautiful friendship. We are still friends, right?"

I smile back at him. "Of course, Denver. We'll always be friends if that's what you really want." We eat our pie in silence. I glance down at my watch. "Time's up, Denver. I've got to get back. Where are you headed next?"

His signature grin pops out at me and leaves me a little breathless, like always. "Wherever life takes me, I guess. Would you give me one last ride for old time's sake?"

I'm confused. "To where?"

He winks. "Just up the road a few miles."

We walk out together. He climbs in the passenger seat, rolls down the window, and says nothing. His silence drives me crazy. I head down the highway in the opposite direction of home. We roll over a few hills. We pop over the next one. There's a huge field of dandelions. "Stop! Pull over." I slow the car down and get over on the shoulder. He looks out the window for a few minutes. I wait patiently. He turns back to me and frames my face with his hands. As my heart breaks, I lean in for one last kiss. Tears roll down my face. He pulls away, wiping my tears. "Remember me, Ciara."

I nod my head and give him a small, defeated smile. "How could I forget you?"

He places something in my hand. "I got you a track phone, for just a little while. That way you'll know it's me."

I nod. "But you have my other number."

He smiles. "I know, but I'd like to think you have something that belongs to only me."

"Thanks." I grab the bag from the back seat and chuck it in his lap. "Here's something that belongs to only me. I think you'll find it quite memorable." I blush as I look away and wait for him to open the sack.

He laughs out loud. "You *really* want to give me this?" I turn to face him. My face goes beet red as he holds my red bra up in the air. I nod my head, unable to speak. I stare at him again. I can hardly believe I've made Denver Evans blush, but that's what's happening, as he shakes his head back and forth, holding my bra like it's a foreign object.

I can't believe I find my voice. "If you want to keep it, you'll have to put it back in the bag." He moves as if on auto pilot, shoving it back in there and staring straight ahead. I turn my head sideways, muttering, "It's just a bra."

He reaches over and touches my arm. I feel instant heat as I turn back to him. "You didn't see what I did, Ciara. You were so hot, standing on the rocks by the river, with the moonlight on your skin." He stops a second and just sits there. "So hot." His words are almost reverent, and I want so badly to believe them, but even more, I want him to stay. I look at him. His jaw is set, and I know nothing's going to change his mind. I can't help but smile. In some ways, we are the same.

He turns and hops out of the car. I feel lost as he walks with a slight limp on his sore ankle around the front of my car. His face hovers over my open window, and I look up at him in question as he smiles down at me. "This is it, then." He looks past me through the car. "That's a perfect field of dandelions to be left in."

My heart lurches at the memory of our silly conversation, and I can't believe he remembers. "You remembered."

His face gets all serious. "I remember everything you've ever said to me, Ciara. From the very first day."

Desperation kicks in, and I feel weak as I try to change his mind. "Denver, be serious. I'm not going to just leave you on the side of the road beside a bunch of dandelions because of something I said."

He sighs and gives me a shy smile. "Ciara, this is my life. I'd be stuck if I tried to stay here. I'm not like you. I don't have a choice. I have to move on." There's anger and frustration in his tone. I feel like he's not hearing me.

My heart breaks as I answer. "There's always two choices in life, Denver. There's a right choice, and there's a wrong one. Make the right one. Come back with me. Please."

He stares out at the road and leans on my window. "The right choice for you isn't the right one for me. I love you, Ciara, as much as I can love anyone, but it's not enough to keep me here. There's a wildness inside me, a need to see new places and try new things. I can't do that here. I need to go."

My heart breaks a little. I've lost him. "I'll miss you, Denver Evans. Life won't be the same without you." I stare down at my steering wheel. "I won't be the same without you."

His hand goes under my chin, nudging it gently upwards. "Keep your chin up, Ciara. Never let anyone make you question your worth. Be strong. Be bold. Be who you are meant to be."

My eyes fly to his face, frustrated. "Take your own advice, Evans."

He chuckles. "Easier said than done, Yengst." He stands up from his hunkering over my window, turns away from me as he faces traffic and sticks out his thumb. I know I've lost him for good. He speaks into the wind. "Life isn't always black and white, Ciara. I've got to move on. I can't go back to where I was, but you can. Go home to your family and write our story with Alex."

I gaze at his back. I memorize the hard and unforgiving edges of Denver and wonder who I am as I drive away, leaving him stranded on the side of the road. He grows smaller and smaller in my rearview mirror, but the bottomless hole in my heart grows larger.

I call Char on the track phone. I need her strength so I don't go back to him.

"Ciara?" Her concern reaches through the phone, giving me strength.

"Hey, Char."

"Ciara, what number is this? Are you okay?"

I breathe out and wait for her lecture, but there's only silence as I answer. "No, but I'm going to be."

epilogue

I n the end, Stella's story was written by Alex Smith, and the part I played was in there, but I chose to remain anonymous.

As for me and Denver, our story is written on my heart, and that's good enough for me. Denver will always be uncharted territory; irreplaceable and exciting, but there are consequences for playing with fire.

For now, I choose to be happy being an ordinary girl living an ordinary life. Climbing mountains can be treacherous, unpredictable, and overrated. As Char loves to say; "You're young. You've got your whole life ahead of you. There's plenty of time to pick dandelions and get lost in the woods."

———

Available Spring 2022
Rough Terrain
All or Nothing #2

———

Don't miss your next favorite book!

Join the Fire & Ice mailing list
www.fireandiceya.com/mail.html